M000021319

For THE BOYHOOD CLUB

Larry Tyle

Dick Piland

Ken Robinson

Jim Fleming

"TEMPUS FUGIT!"

For Bud &
Barbara!
Aloha & Mahalo!
Ron Toney
7/13/12

ACKNOWLEDGEMENTS

With many thanks to my editor, Kate Haas, for her sharp eye and pencil. And a special thanks to my wife, Linnette, for her willingness to live with the unfolding of this story, reading it through at least twice, and for her willingness to live with me for fifty-one years.

CHAPTER 1

The inimitable Candi Summers, Gordie Nockers' star dancer, stared blankly up through the smoky haze of the strip joint into the strobe lights reflecting and circling above and around her. She bore her pelvis down deeper and harder, deeper and harder, into Old Mel's lap, the heavy metal rock music driving her on. She yawned as Old Mel's skinny face looked up at her, his eyes misted with hope and expectation.

"Push down harder, God-damn it, push harder," he muttered. His hands groped around her waist and he grabbed at her rear-end, his arthritic fingers digging in.

"Keep your dirty, fucking hands off my ass," she yelled in his ear, causing painful feedback to his hearing aid, though it was barely audible above the din of the nightclub. Candi smiled blandly at the men gathered around, staring at her, their faces glistening with anticipation in the dim, reflected light of the bar.

What a way to earn a living, she thought, lap dancing for a roomful of shitheels and assholes. She knuckled herself deeper and deeper into Old Mel's crotch, gyrating around and around, while Old Mel, ecstatically, fumblingly, stuck dollar bills into her bra, his hands fluttering like gnarled birds across her chest.

"And don't try and slip that old knob into me, you bastard." She'd had them try that one many times before. One old logger from Estacada almost had his dick snapped off one night when, in the throes of her performance and his desire, she slipped off his lap accidentally and they both went flying from the bar stool to the

1

floor. Poor Gordie Nockers almost had a heart attack over that one, fearful that some legal beagle was sitting nearby, ready to pounce. "Keep it in your pants where it belongs," she warned.

Nockers' Up-Town Bar and Grille was crowded with the usual array of horny drunks, construction workers, cops and college boys out on the town. It was a weekend and it was party time. The college boys were easy to spot, with their embarrassed grins, sweaty hands, meager tips, and often their forged IDs. Yes, it was a Saturday night and Candi was in good form and pulling in the dollar bills, one after another. An English major at East Hills Liberty College, hoping for a career as a writer of Christian romance, she did what she could to make ends meet. Her folks still lived in the small town in eastern Oregon where she had grown up, and she was now making her own way in the Big City. East Hills Liberty College was a small church-run school. It had let her enroll without too many questions being asked other than whether or not she had been "saved". Of course, she assured them, she had been. Student loans paid for much of her tuition, but beyond that, she was on her own. Her folks didn't have much to contribute. If they could only see me now, she thought. Her parents knew nothing of her present occupation and thought she was working swing shift as an aide in a nursing home. Old Mel had a pleased look on his face as he pushed his last buck into her bikini panties, trying his best to get a feel of the "promised land." But Candi was too quick for him. They had all tried that one on her. Old Mel made one final desperate lunge and then the music ended. They all wanted their money's worth, Candi thought, and more, if they could get it. From her, they couldn't get it. She was the star of the bar and she didn't come easy. She grabbed the bill from his groping fingers, transferred it quickly and expertly to her bra and disappeared into the dressing room in the back. From the back of the bar the blaring music had reached its climax, along with, perhaps, Old Mel, and his hard-on began to deflate. Clouds of cigarette smoke drifted in dead layers above her, floating on the stagnant air, filtered only by the darkness of the room. And now the lonely and solitary men at the bar and seated at the small round tables turned once again to their beer and peanuts, waiting for the next dance to begin, for the next tired looking girl, barely clothed, to appear in the footlights and strut onto the runway that stretched across the back of the bar, and to begin wrapping herself around the shiny metal pole that reached up through the layers of smoke to the ceiling.

Candi sat alone in the back room counting her take for the set. $53.10. Gordie Nockers, her boss, had left for the evening, his head pounding with yet another migraine. His wife, Ophelia Nockers, was out front tending the bar. Candi stared at the dime in her hand. Ten cents? What cheap son of a bitch put that in there? Disgusted, she turned the coin over in her hand then threw it into an ashtray in the center of the table, the one they used to collect parking meter change. Still, fifty-three dollors wasn't bad for a half hour of dry-humping some old fart's johnson.

Big Cal, Gordie's oversized bouncer, walked in. She looked up at him and smiled.

He watched her as she dressed, his eyes enjoying the intimacy of his own private performance as she casually prepared to go home to her apartment. He might as well have been one of the fixtures, as far as the girls at Nockers' were concerned. None of them exhibited any modesty in his presence. Dumb as he was, he knew why. It had nothing to do with the fact that they stripped for money before crowds of strangers. It was that they didn't really know he existed. At least, not in the ways he would have liked.

He was "Big Cal" to the girls. Cal was born to be a bouncer. And little else. A big brute, he came by his nickname honestly. It was probably one of the few things he came by honestly. At 350 pounds, if he weighed an ounce, his shaved head perpetually beaded with sweat, a dark, scraggly goatee gracing his chin, enough fat on his gut to feed China, no one not stoned out of his mind would ever think to mess with Big Cal. When he hired Cal, Gordie

Nockers had told Ophelia, that if he'd had a dog with a face half as ugly as Cal's he'd shave his ass and teach him to walk backwards.

"You goin' out for another set?" Cal asked.

"Nah. I've had it for tonight. $223 for an evening's work. Plus ten cents." Candi grinned impishly. Cal soaked it in. Slowly she pulled on her street clothes over her bra and panties, traded her spiked heels for a pair of sandals, brushed back her long, dark hair and got ready to leave.

Candi slipped Cal a twenty as she opened the side door. "See ya tomorrow night." Cal pocketed the cash and watched as she stepped out into the darkness of the parking lot, still packed with mostly junker cars and pick-up trucks. It was a warm evening, mid-June. The music and cigarette smoke seemed to trail out the door after her. He stood watching until he was certain she had reached the safety of her car.

He heard the motor chug to life, saw the headlights come on and the taillights begin to glow. He slowly turned and closed the door as her aging VW crept out of the parking lot into the late night traffic and quickly disappeared down the street and into the darkened corridors of Oregon City.

CHAPTER 2

A "TITTY" BAR! IT COULDN'T GET ANY BETTER THAN THAT. FOR MOST of his life Gordon Nockers had disliked his surname intensely. In fact, it had been the bane of his existence, especially starting with his high school years. Sometimes he wished his grandfather hadn't changed it from the respectable old-country name "Nokowitsky" when he immigrated to America in the early 1900s. Surely the old man had never realized what a burden the Anglicized version of that name would be for his descendents. And in particular, for poor Gordie Nockers. He had been the butt of every joke imaginable. That is, until several years ago when he had the good sense and good fortune to buy the run-down site of a former Denny's restaurant and rename it Nockers' Up-Town Bar and Grille. At first business was very slow, but buying the place turned out to be the best move he had ever made. Ophelia Nockers, his ever patient and adoring wife, even approved when he got the bright idea of turning the place into a "titty" bar - then the money began to roll in. That was long before the entrancing Candi Summers went to work there as a stripper.

In the years since he had opened Nockers' Up-Town Bar and Grille, Gordon had changed the format very little. Why tamper with success? Nude dancing - pole, stage and table - was the main-stay of the entertainment, along with watered-down drinks and micro-waved bar food. There had been fads from time to time, and he had tried them all, including wrestling matches between two well-endowed naked women in a vat of Jello. This had come to a sudden and disgusting end when one of the girls accidentally slipped on a blackened slice of banana that had sunk to the bottom of the pit (part of the Jello salad concoction being used on that particular night) and cracked her skull open. The State had stepped in with a Workman's Compensation claim, along with the local health authorities who threatened to close him down). There had also been an animal act in which a chimp wearing pasties and a G string twirled around on stage to tunes from an early Monkees' album. That effort also ended badly when the chimp bit an overzealous near-sighted customer who then sued big time, seeking damages for injuries both physical and emotional. Gordie's insurance carrier told him the chimp had to go.

But generally business was good, especially with the local college boys, the nearby construction workers and the constant stream of conventioneers in their out-dated leisure suits who arrived each day from the Holiday Inn up the street. The girls worked their hearts out. Big Cal kept order. Ophelia Nockers kept her close and steady eye on the till. And Gordon spent most of the time in his cramped little office in the backroom of the bar, smoking the occasional stogie and trying to shut out the constantly blaring noise of the gigantic stereo system he had installed. Lately, his migraines were kicking in more and more frequently, and he needed increasingly prodigious amounts of vicodin more and more often to keep them in check. The downside of this business was that you could never get away from it. Take a day off and the help would steal you blind. Or a pastie would pop off a dancer's boob and hit a customer in the eye or land in his drink. (There would inevitably be a trial lawyer sitting next to him at the bar ready to hand out his card.) A high heel could break. A G string could get entangled in some dancer's delicate underpinnings and you would have a girl sobbing on your shoulder or, worse yet, quitting just before she was scheduled to go on. Or the very worst of all, it could suddenly be "that time of the month" for your star attraction. An occupational hazard.

Finding dancers was no problem, however. Gordon got a lot of his "talent" from a private college nearby. East Hills Liberty College was a church-affiliated school on the outskirts of Oregon City with a high number of women students from small towns scattered across Oregon and Southwest Washington. These students were living in the big city for the first time in their lives, and all of them needed to support themselves. There just wasn't enough money in sheep ranching anymore to cover both their tuition and room and board, even with financial aid. Few of the girls could actually dance, or had experience with establishments like Nockers' Up-Town Bar and Grille; but they all knew how to take their clothes off and sway to the music. It didn't take long to piece together an act that was good enough for the customers of Nockers'. And it was relatively easy money, so long as Big Cal kept the customers off the girls. At least the customers with no money left to spend.

True, there had been some arrests over the years. Now and then, a girl would take a customer up on his proposition for something more than a table dance. Gordon did his best to discourage that sort of thing, since he was at heart a good, God-fearing, born-again Christian himself, who went to church each Sunday and left an ample contribution in the offering plate. But it happened from time to time. The vice cops tended to hang around to see what was going on, and Gordon saw to it that they got the best of everything, and often on the house. Cops all loved the Titty bars. There were times that Nockers' was so crowded with cops that it looked like a precinct. They'd gather around the stage in their street clothes, off duty, drinks in hand, gawking at each new dancer as she made her appearance, cheering her on and placing bets on the measurements of her chest.

Yes, all in all Nockers' Up-Town Bar and Grille had been a great success for Gordon. And he had just learned that he had been elected by his fellow business owners in Oregon City to assume the position of president of the local Chamber of Commerce for the coming year. It couldn't get any better than that.

CHAPTER 3

CANDI'S APARTMENT WAS UP THE HILL ABOVE OREGON CITY, THE county seat for Clackamas County, a large but not heavily populated county just south of the urban area of Portland. Candi's place was about five miles from the bar and close to the college campus, which made it convenient for her, if not luxurious or even particularly comfortable. It was dank and gloomy as usual when Candi pushed her way inside. An older, two-story wood-frame U-shaped building, she had the end unit on the ground floor. She lived alone, a boy friend, Jesse, the latest in a line of boyfriends over the past several years, now gone. She had kicked him out a few weeks ago for failure to contribute to the expenses, abusiveness, and drug use.

What remained of her dinner was still on the kitchen table, next to the textbooks she had been studying before leaving for the club. It was hot and stuffy in the apartment and flies were circling the crusted plates. Crap, she thought, as she cleared the dishes and put them in the sink. I've got to clean this dump up one of these days. Maybe after final exams are over. She ran some water over the plates and left them to soak. The air was close and silent. There was no sound but the whir and chattering of a fan coming from the apartment immediately above. A substitute for air-conditioning. It was hot and muggy. This summer is going to be a scorcher, Candi thought. She didn't even own a fan.

She went into the bathroom and ran hot bath water. A good, long soak will take away some of the stink of the bar, and all the old coots like Old Mel, she thought. She slowly stripped off her clothes and soon was lying stretched out in the tub, the warm water sloshing over her body and soothing her aching pelvis. At last she began to relax and unwind. Now that Jesse was gone, she had to admit that she was lonely at times. At least he had been company. At times. At other times he was just another free-loading, glassed out, abusive pain in the ass. Mostly that, she decided. She stared up at the mottled, flaking ceiling, at the lighting fixture that always swayed precariously whenever her upstairs neighbor, a religion major at the college who liked to practice his preacher moves at all hours, clomped around from one room to another, pretending he was preaching to the masses in a mega-church somewhere and shouting "Hallelujah" and "God be praised." Christ, she thought, that thing is going to fall down one of these days and kill me. Quickly she stepped from the tub, toweled off and looked at herself in the steamy mirror. Despite her tawdry work at the club, a twenty-two year-old's expression of relative innocence stared back at her. She smiled. Still got it, she thought. Time to hit the books.

Curled up on her bed Candi carefully studied her English literature text for Monday's final exam, trying to anticipate what Professor Kees would be asking. For a brief moment she thought about Professor Kees himself, thought of him as a man and not just as a teacher. She had been attracted to him from the first class session. He seemed so sophisticated. She wondered if he ever came to the club. Had she ever danced on his lap? Sometimes she worked without really looking at the poor jerk whose lap she was mangling. As long as the dollar bills were being stuffed into her thong, she couldn't care less whose lap it was. But no; not Professor Kees. She would have recognized him. He was tall and slim, reasonably good looking, for an older man, in a shopworn sort of way. He was always dressed in a saggy tweed sport coat with leather patches on the elbows. Sometimes he even smoked a pipe to make himself seem more mature and intellectual. And she was certain he wore a hairpiece to cover up a balding crown. Sometimes in class he would unconsciously pat his head to make sure it was still in place. He must be at least thirty-five, she thought. Happily married, no doubt. She had remembered seeing a photo on the desk in his office of a rather sullen looking woman, who appeared to be about his age, an average looking woman, with short, brown hair and a reluctant smile, and no make-up. But there were no photos of children.

Candi returned to her studies. Final exams would be here all too soon. She could never remember which was Keats and which was Yeats. Given the spellings, why didn't their names rhyme? After all, they were supposed to be poets.

The cell phone beside her bed chirped. Crap, she thought, looking up at the clock. Jesse's name popped up on the caller ID.

"Yeah, what do you want?" She leaned back against the headboard of the queen-sized bed and glared up at the ceiling. In the apartment above, the future minister was reaching the climax of his sermon for the day.

"It's me," said Jesse, his voice sounding a bit desperate and pleading. "What 'cha doin'?"

"What do you care? I'm studying for finals." She paused. "Besides, it's late." She was ready to hang up. "What do you want?" As if she didn't know. It was either money or pussy. Or both.

"I'm needin' a little," he said. His voice was plaintive and hoarse. She could tell he'd been drinking, or worse yet, was stoned again.

"Needin' a little!" Candi exploded. "You shit-heel. Go down to the bar and pay for it like the rest of the assholes. I'm off duty."

She pushed the end button and the line went dead. Jesse has his nerve, she thought. She was glad to be rid of him. It had been like having a spoiled kid around. Only this one happened to be a stoner and a drunk over six feet tall and twenty-five years old. She put her book aside, turned and flicked off the lamp at her bedside. The room went black. The only sound came from the monotonous rattle of the fan upstairs. And then the religion major's voice broke through the silence once again. Now he was practicing the benediction.

"Shut the fuck up," she yelled up into the darkness. The fan and the benediction abruptly stopped.

CHAPTER 4

JESSE WAS STILL GRUMBLING TO HIMSELF AS HE SNAPPED SHUT HIS CELL phone. "God damn, but she's a mean bitch," he said out loud to no one in particular, as there was no one to hear him. He was alone, as usual, here in his room at the Double Six Motel just off McNary Street, just past the railroad tracks. The curtain was pulled back from the window, and the neon sign over the front office blinked red and blue designs across the worn carpet and up the far wall. Jesse cracked open another beer from the six-pack at his side. He flicked the remote at the aging television set perched on top of the dresser on the other side of the room.

The screen sputtered into life. A replay of a Portland Trailblazer basketball game from several seasons ago was being rebroadcast. Portland was losing. Again. They couldn't win even in the reruns, Jesse thought. He slugged down his beer and took another, opened it, and lay back on the bed. He had been drinking all evening. In fact, he had been drinking most of the day. To top it off, he was slightly red from some not so good meth he'd managed to score earlier. Since he had lost his job at the paper mill and was no longer working, this was his life. Unemployment checks. Beer, meth. The occasional eight-ball. Rockin' chair money, booze and drugs. He had been living at the motel ever since Candi had kicked him out of the apartment. He paid by the week for the room, which came with a basic microwave oven, a small "beer" fridge under the bathroom countertop, a shower stall, a toilet that ran constantly, the barely functional TV and a double bed. The management was thrilled to have a semi-permanent guest, even one of Jesse's relatively dubious character. Most rooms at the Double Six rented out by the hour.

Jesse pulled off his boots and lay back down on the bed. In the rerun of the game J.R. Rider, a much touted guard for the Blazers at that time, had committed yet another turnover; the San Antonio Spurs were running wild, scoring at will. "Bench the asshole," Jesse yelled at the TV, forgetting for the moment that the game had actually been played several seasons ago. J.R. Rider had long ago been shipped off to another team. Shit, I could use a woman, he thought, as he took another deep draw on his beer, almost draining the stubby. If he hadn't lost his driver's license six months ago on that DUI, he thought, he'd get into his pick-up truck and go find one. But he was already on probation. If he got picked up again it would mean jail time for sure. He'd done that before. He had no desire to do it again. With his luck, he'd get stopped for a missing taillight or expired tags. And he couldn't afford to frequent the ladies who hung around the motel. They wanted money, not charm.

Damn, Candi, he thought. Why did she have to go and shit-can him? He'd been good to her. Better than she deserved. He had hardly ever hit her. He had even stopped, for a while, his life of crime, small time as it was. Oh, there was still the occasional shoplift, the five-finger discount. Cigarettes, a six-pack of beer. The usual stuff. Everybody does that. He'd sold some crank from time to time. A little grass. He had to survive, for shit's sake. But nothin' heavy. No bank robberies. He had never kicked in a gas station. He didn't even own a gun anymore. He wasn't up for anything that carried hard time in the crowbar hotel down in Salem. She thinks she's too good for me, he thought. That's really it - college girl and all. I bet she thinks she's goin' to find some college guy on his way to being a doctor or a lawyer. Somebody to take care of her in style for the rest of her life. He sneered as Rider made yet another error and inadvertently tossed the ball to David Robinson, the San Antonio center, who ran the length of the floor for an easy and thunderous dunk, making the backboard rattle to the hometown crowd's dismay. They hissed and booed.

Jesse groaned too. It was getting late. In the front office, the pimply faced desk clerk, a Bible student from the college who was working the night shift, flipped off the overhead neon sign. Jesse's room suddenly lost all color; nothing but the flickering glare of the black and white television set illuminating the dreariness. He sank deeper into the threadbare pillow. Women, he thought. Life. God, it all sucks. He still felt a little twitchy from the meth. He set the empty beer bottle on the floor beside the bed, now part of a neat row of brown bottles stretching out into the middle of the room. He pulled back the covers on the bed, removed his pants and slid between what had in some prior life been sheets. The Blazers had miraculously made a comeback and come within one point of the Spurs. With no time remaining on the clock, Rider had been fouled while driving to the basket for a lay-in, which he had missed. It was his chance to be a hero. He clanked the first of two free throws off the front of the basket rim. The crowd moaned. Then held its collective breath for the second shot. Rider could still at least tie the score and send the game into overtime. But no, he clanked that shot off the iron too. The Rose Garden was deadly quiet. The game was over. Like mourners at a funeral, the crowd filed silently out of the building and headed for home - or a local bar.

Disgusted, Jesse flicked off the TV set, plunging the room into total darkness. Where was Candi when he really needed her? Or someone? Or anyone? Alone as he was, he now curled himself up into a fetal position. Reaching down between his legs, he grabbed his cock to console himself. Ah, at least there was always man's best friend.

CHAPTER 5

CANDI'S GIVEN NAME WAS ACTUALLY CANDICE. BUT SHE HATED THAT; it sounded so prudish to her. She had been called "Perky" for a time, a shortened form of her middle name, Priscilla. But she didn't like that name either. She wasn't "perky," so far as she was concerned, and she didn't want to project that image of herself. So she ended up "Candi" because it was a natural nickname and was what the other kids at school always called her. She started dancing at the club as "Candi," and one night one of the old guys, one of the regulars, suggested to his cohorts with a smirk on his grizzled face, that she must have gotten her nickname because she liked to suck on "hard candy," and he went on to say that he had just the "hard candy" for her to suck on. He snickered when he said it. Candi overheard.

"It's not "Candi" for anything," she muttered to him as she reached down and fiercely twisted his nuts into a soft pretzel. Doubled over in agony, he acknowledged as much as he vainly tried to extricate himself from her iron grip. She was strong for such a slip of a thing. No one at the club ever bothered her or made fun of her name again, so she decided to continue to go by "Candi." And Gordie loved it.

Candi's parents, however, disliked her nickname intensely, and did all they could to discourage its use. The family lived in a small, eastern Oregon town, and they were convinced that Candice was a true, God-given name, denoting a sense of purity and righteousness, whereas "Candi" was somehow suggestive of the work of the devil.

No good could come from a name like that. Consequently, as long as she continued to live at home, in church every Sunday morning and evening and every Wednesday night at prayer services, it was always "Candice". But during the rest of the week, at school, and among her friends, however, she was simply Candi. Even Pastor Fairly, the rather rotund minister of the small Four Square church the family attended, was compelled to loudly intone "Candice" to the congregation when he doused her in the baptismal fount. It was a full-body plunge, taken when she had just turned fourteen, and he managed to cleverly fondle her budding breasts as he lifted her from the holy water and pronounced her pure in the eyes of the Lord. Pastor Fairly was good at that sort of sleight of hand, and Candi was not the only recipient of his pastoral expressiveness. But she was by far the most developed of his charges and he followed her progress with a keen interest.

Unfortunately, the baptism was not the end of Candi's encounters with Pastor "Bob," as he liked to be called by the young folk in the church, especially the young girls. Two summers later, when she was sixteen, she went to the annual church camp up at Wallowa Lake, high in the heart of the Wallowa Mountains. Late one night, still hungry, she slipped out of her cabin dormitory to find something to eat in the camp pantry. There she happened to meet up with Pastor Bob, who was feeding his own excessive appetites. After a number of warm hugs, all in the name of Jesus, Candi ended up eating more than she had bargained for. Their furtive liaisons continued undetected for another year, including one rather rough ride atop the Pastor's desk in his church office one Sunday morning just after services. On that occasion she had to quickly and indiscriminately sweep a copy of a book of essays Pastor Bob had been reading on the wonders of the Book of Revelations to the floor in order to make a place on the desk for her rear end. The good pastor, having just served Communion to his flock, did not seem to notice this affront to the Lord in his desire to fill her with the Holy Spirit.

The cherished book of essays fell to the floor, forgotten in a frenzy of overweight passion that followed.

The furtive relationship came to a sudden end when Pastor Bob was suddenly, without announcement to the congregation or ceremony, transferred by the church fathers to an even smaller church in an even smaller town on the Idaho border. There were unkind rumors floating around but never anything specific. Fortunately for Candi, her name was never brought up in connection to the tawdry affair. She was quite certain that her father would have gut-shot Pastor Bob if he had known. Pastor Bob was replaced by Pastor Quinlan, a tall, gangly older man with a long, wispy strand of gray hair that wound around his otherwise bald head like a halo. He was not nearly as attentive to Candi as Pastor Bob had been, and seemed oblivious to either her salvation or her emerging womanhood.

Several years later, after Candi had graduated from high school and moved to the big city to pursue her formal higher education, she encountered Pastor Bob once again attending an ecclesiastical conference at the East Hills Liberty College. In his desire to have a better understanding of the horrors of the life of sin in larger cities he allowed himself to slink into Nockers' Up-Town Bar and Grille under cover of darkness. Pastor Bob was apparently unaware that Candi was part of the entertainment package he was researching on God's behalf, and she found herself gyrating on his bulging lap like a whirling dervish. In the hazy lighting of the bar, she did not recognize him. Her attention was perhaps diverted by the Day-Glo painting of a naked lady on his wide necktie that gleamed and rippled up and down his chest and across his stomach in the rotating beams of the strobe lights above them. It might have been thought to be an unusual fashion statement for a Man of the Cloth. As did the loudly checkered leisure suit that had not been in style since the 70s. In any event, he did not apparently recognize her either, or, if he did, did not so indicate. Which may have accounted for his apparent lack of generosity. The two one dollar bills he hesitantly and somewhat reluctantly stuck in her bra when the music stopped seemed a small offering, indeed, for such a spirited performance. Perhaps, he may just have felt compelled as a messenger of God not to reward her for her sinning in such an open and notorious fashion. Or perhaps he did recognize her and felt he ought not to have to now pay for what he had once enjoyed free of charge.

CHAPTER 6

BIG CAL LOCKED UP THE CLUB, SURVEYED THE NEAR EMPTY PARKING lot to see that all the slobs and drunks were really gone, climbed into his old, badly dented, primer-gray Honda Civic and headed for the trailer park where he enjoyed life in a single-wide that, like him, had seen better days. He lived alone, as he had done for years. He had long ago concluded that no woman would ever really want him. At least not as he wanted to be wanted. He spent his working hours watching attractive and semi-attractive young women wiggle and twist their way into men's hearts and pocketbooks. But they all treated him like a big, not too bright, older brother. They laughed with him. They shared the details of their love lives with him. But they never went home with him. They never shared his life away from the club, his real life, in any way.

His work at the strip club was the best job he had ever had. He had always wanted to be a cop when he was a kid. But he lacked the basic education, having dropped out of high school after only one year. He never liked school. He never felt that he fitted into the social life, especially in high school. He was always the biggest kid in the class. Had he been particularly athletic as well as big, he might have been a sports hero on campus. But he wasn't. He was just big. He didn't do well in the classroom. He always felt out of place, the butt of the jokes. He got into a lot of fights and was expelled more times than he could count. Finally one day he never went back. That was the end of that.

Now Cal was so fat across his stomach that even the rent-a-cop outfits didn't want him. He had applied to all of them. But the club had hired him as a bouncer, a peace-keeper, Gordie had called it. And he was good at getting guys out of the place and away from the girls quickly if necessary, and with a minimum of fuss. He was remarkably quick for his size. All it took was a sign of trouble, a nod from one of his girls, and the guy was a goner. Bam! Out the door, on his ass in the parking lot wondering what had happened. And Cal could remember their faces, so that once they had been eighty-sixed, they were banned for life. There were no second chances in Cal's court of law. The word got around and there was very little trouble at Nockers' Up-Town Bar and Grille. Cal took good care of his girls. And they knew it.

It was 2:30 a.m. when Cal parked the old Honda under the carport and found his way to his dark trailer. There were still lights on in a few of the other trailers squeezed side by side in the cramped confines of the park. The rent was cheap and the trailer park was located just a couple of miles from the club. It was quiet as usual and the hot night air pressed in on Big Cal as he entered the trailer. It had all the charm of an abandoned cliff dwelling. A visitor might have expected to see carvings and primitive paintings on the walls. He hurriedly snatched a warm beer from the cupboard, opened it with one hand and turned on the TV set hoping to catch the closing half hour of a rerun of the Larry Singer Talk Show. Tonight's show featured a bi-sexual chiropractor who had left a long term marriage with a hyperactive stock broker for a midget wrestler named Tanya. The two had met when he was attending the pro wrestling matches one night in Eureka, California, and Tanya had been thrown from the ring right into his lap and had dislocated her hip. The chiropractor fixed her up on the spot and the rest was history.

Cal had seen it before, several times in fact. It was one of his favorites. He sat down and watched as an array of odd balls, the Chiropractor, the midget wrestler and the spurned wife, paraded across the stage threatening one another, and the audience, made up of folks who looked very much like him and many of his neighbors, was shouting obscenities that were being bleeped out, and hissing at them, making lewd gestures that were purposely out of focus to protect the purity of the viewing public, and challenging the guests to a fight. Cal had always wanted to someday be part of the show. He even had a publicity photo of Larry Singer on the wall of his bedroom. He had been told that it had been signed by Larry himself.

By 3:00 a. m. the show had reached its climax and conclusion and, drained by the drama of it all, Cal slumped into the bedroom, a freshly opened bottle of beer in his hand. The club opened at noon on Sundays and Cal had to be there. The action didn't usually pick up until later, especially on Sundays, but there were always the usual few early drunks who needed a drink badly enough that they came trooping in as soon as the neon sign went on and the door was unlocked. Above all else, he needed to be there to take care of his girls. Especially Candi, his favorite. He felt a special bond with her. Yeah, she was a college girl and all, but unlike some of the others, she never acted snooty, or treated him like a piece of the furniture. He liked the fact that she was from a small, rural town. She didn't put on airs. He was certain she probably watched the Larry Singer Show too, but he had never asked her about that.

He pulled back the covers and lowered his massive weight onto the cot that served as a bed. Soon he was dreaming his favorite dream. He was right there, on the Larry Singer Show. Candi was whirling her cute little ass around and around on his lap. "Cal, be mine, be mine," she kept murmuring in his ear as the music played louder and louder and the crowd roared its approval. In the dark of the old trailer he smiled his best Larry Singer smile. He could almost see the two of them on stage live, right there in good old Hollywood, California, the cameras rolling, the hot lights glaring down, the unruly crowd cheering them on. It would be heaven.

CHAPTER 7

RUSSELL KEES LOOKED UP FROM THE FINAL EXAM HE WAS PREPARING FOR his bonehead English literature class and gazed soulfully out his small window at the campus quad below, now mostly deserted. Actually, all his courses were bonehead literature classes. That's all East Hills Liberty College really offered by way of either classes or students. Russell was alone in his campus office. He had compiled some fifty multiple-choice questions. That was plenty for this class. Most of these kids were so dense and unimaginative that it would take them the entire two hours to complete it. Some of them wouldn't even make it then. Most of these students weren't bright enough to try and cheat. That was one thing he could take for granted with them. There goes the week, he thought. Then I have to grade the damn things. He looked at the photo of the woman on his desk staring up at him and he stared back. Fortunately Mrs. Kees was off to Mt. Vernon, Washington visiting with and caring for her elderly parents, now in poor and diminishing health. She would be traveling back and forth over the course of the entire summer vacation, and perhaps beyond, spending the bulk of her time on nursing duties. The upside of his wife's absence for Russell was that, with college out of session for the summer, Russell would have the house to himself a good part of the time. There was no apparent downside to all this that he could see. He looked forward to the solitude. It would give him a chance to perhaps finish that novel that lay dormant in the lower drawer of his desk. He had been trying to develop a good Christian plot for it but so far it had eluded him. He secretly preferred the drama of mayhem and rape to charity and good works. He assumed his potential readers might too. As well as certain potential publishers. Perhaps he should write about the Inquisition. That could get juicy. He wasn't quite sure how to work a delicate sex scene into it, however. Sex was tricky for these Christians.

Russell thought back over his relatively brief career teaching students at the church-affiliated college the great works of literature, expurgated, of course, to protect the innocent, with the occasional poetry workshop thrown in. That he had had two poems published in the campus literary magazine, *Heavenly Discourse*, qualified him in the eyes of the administration as the "Poet in Residence" here. "*Ode to the Salvation of a Woodcock*" had been especially gratifying. Yes, his career here had not been what he had hoped it would be or expected. It had seemed that his month-long on-line course through the MFA program at the diploma mill in Van Nuys, California had hardly been worthwhile. It had cost him five hundred dollars, plus the printing costs for the diploma itself. At the thought of the diploma, he looked up admiringly at the large and colorfully designed certificate of matriculation that hung framed on the wall across from his desk, positioned so that visiting students would readily see it. It was there alongside his Certificate of Attendance at the College of English Arts out of Boring, Oregon. CARNEGIE MELON UNIVERSITY, it read. MASTER OF FINE ARTS, Creative Writing, RUSSELL WILBUR KEES. It looked impressive, which was all that mattered to the administration, and so far no one had noticed or at least commented on the fact that the spelling of "Melon" differed from that of the prestigious Carnegie Mellon University. But then, few of his students and few of his colleagues could read that well, or would have known the difference. And the lighting in his office was rather dim. An appropriate metaphor, he thought.

Nevertheless Russell felt good about himself despite the drawbacks of teaching at a college like East Hills Liberty, which included not only many dull, rather mindless students, and colorless colleagues, but also the prison-like structures that surrounded him. While the pay was not particularly good, the benefits included health care and a small IRA plan, and in addition he had this tiny office to himself, tucked away as it was on the third floor of one of the nondescript, gray concrete buildings that characterized the architecture of East Hills Liberty. An aerial shot of East Hills Liberty College could easily have been mistaken for a state penitentiary. One almost expected to see gun towers at each corner of the campus, poised to mow down escapees if necessary. Russell didn't give a rat's ass for the religious orientation of the school, or the goody, goody students it tended to attract. Or the fact that it lacked any kind of acceptable accreditation by any known agency that evaluated institutions of higher education. It had been accredited by the John the Baptist Council of the Saved, a small gathering of independent fundamentalist churches based in Kansas, and that was good enough for the administration and, for the most part, for the students who chose to attend East Hills. Russell played the game well, and that was what counted here. He could look as pious as anyone else when it mattered, such as at mid-week campus prayer meetings, or at the Sunday morning, "Praise the Lord" services, and the Sunday evening potluck. Attendance was required at these functions under his yearly contract. Of course, the bottom line for Russell was that no other college teaching positions were available for someone with his lack of verifiable credentials.

Yes, all in all, he felt okay about himself as he surveyed again Monday's exam questions. "Do not go gentle into that good night." Who wrote that line?

A. Jewel

B. Dylan Thomas

C. George W. Bush (his little effort at humor)

D. Bob Dylan

What is the form of the poem?

A. Sonnet

B. Villanelle

C. Haiku

D. Limerick

He always liked to throw in a ringer now and then just to keep them on their toes.

Some of the students were, no doubt, a bit suspicious of anyone who knew such worldly terms as Villanelle, terms not found in the Bible. However, some of the young ladies, he thought, almost seemed to swoon over him at times in the old fashioned, Beatlemania sort of way. He was as close to a local celebrity as East Hills Liberty was ever going to have. After all, he was a published poet. There was just a hint of naughtiness about him.

One student in particular, Candi Summers, a comely young thing, athletic and strong looking, but still sweet and pretty, had especially attracted his attention. She was in his English literature class and would be taking this very exam. He had noticed her peeking at him from time to time over the top of her textbook when she thought he wasn't looking. He occasionally, in fact, got a quick clam shot whenever she would spread her legs while slipping out from her desk at the end of class, wearing an especially short skirt. He found himself anxiously awaiting the end of each session, as were most of his students as well. But for different reasons. The sight of her for three hours each week almost made teaching here worthwhile, even though he realized that East Hills Liberty might well be the end of the road, so far as his teaching career was concerned.

Still he knew with the end of spring term and summer now on the way, once exams were over, graded and grades turned in, he would be free to pursue his creative self. He had contracted to teach a poetry workshop at God+Write, the annual Christian writing conference held at Wallowa Lake each summer. He was looking forward to the opportunity to relax in the refreshing clear air of the high mountains of Northeastern Oregon, aptly known locally as the Switzerland of America. Spending most of the month of July up there would be just what he needed to recharge his creative batteries. Meanwhile poor Lucy would be stuck at Mt. Vernon most of the summer tending to her fading and cranky parents. What a shame.

Russell sighed as he pushed the "Start" button and copies of the final exam began rolling out of the printer. It was Sunday evening. Now that Lucy was gone perhaps he should get out of the house for a while. He would attend to his Sunday evening duties at the college potluck and then he could slip out and perhaps enjoy a quiet drink somewhere where the administration would not see him. Of course, East Hills Liberty did not approve of alcohol. Or much of anything else. At least not officially. *Do not go gentle into that good night,* he thought. Maybe George W. Bush did write that after all. If he didn't, he probably should have.

CHAPTER 8

Viktor Karshenko was late again for class. He had rushed from his small, rented house near the campus of Orel Robarts Bible College, but, as usual, was tardy. However, he knew that his students would wait for him. They always did. Today they had no real choice in the matter. It was the day of final examinations. He lugged his heavy briefcase, his soft, pudgy frame struggling with the overload of books and materials for his Russian literature class. It was not easy for a man of his advanced years. But it was June, his favorite month. Classes would soon be over for the school year and to his relief he would not be teaching summer sessions, a relief, since he had done so every year since he had arrived seven years ago at this most unlikely of all places, the Ozark Mountains, to teach at Orel Robarts.

There were not many students in his Russian lit class. Only fourteen, to be exact. Russian literature, or literature of any kind, except for the King James Version of the Bible, was not of great interest to the kind of students who chose to come to Orel Robarts Bible College. Robarts trained students, if "trained" was the right word, to go out into the world and bring lost souls to Jesus. Never mind whatever their other needs or adversities might be, such as poverty or war, but saving their souls was a high priority. They were missionaries at heart. Enriching their minds with literature was not normally part of the objective. Or the fine arts. Or music, other than, perhaps, some Christian rock. However, for some reason, the administration thought some exposure to literature, as long as it had been properly expurgated of naughtiness or ungodliness, was a necessary part of the school's curriculum, since there were state laws affecting their marginal accreditation that seemed to require some such courses. And there was always much desired federal money floating around that was contingent on some sort of broader, albeit, secular view of the world. While they didn't necessarily agree, to put it bluntly, they wanted the money. It all had something to do with being well-rounded. In a nutshell, educated. Thus a course in such areas as Russian literature. Pushkin, Gogol, Turgenev, Tolstoy (especially Tolstoy, as everyone had heard of him). Nothing modern, however, was allowed. Certainly nothing from the communist era.

And, as it turned out, Viktor was just the man to teach such a course. Now well into his seventies, he had been born in Odessa, that cosmopolitan port city of culture and learning on the Black Sea. The Ukraine. The bread basket of Mother Russia. First a province of Russia, then, during Viktor's time there, a part of the Soviet Union, and now, following the breakup of the Union, an independent nation. Though he was Ukrainian, Viktor still thought of himself as Russian at heart. He had later taught in Moscow at a secondary school until, during the height of the Communist regime, the authorities had clamped down on him for teaching the works of Pasternak and Solzhenitsyn, as well as contemporary American writers such as Kurt Vonnegut and Phillip Roth. But it was the publication of his first book of poems that finally sealed his fate. Entitled, *"The Stalin Nightmare,"* it was published surreptitiously under a pseudonym by a small, non-government-controlled press, and distributed from hand to hand by dissidents for months, until it was finally traced to Viktor by the KGB, and he was thrown in jail and then shipped off to Siberia for five years at hard labor.

Eventually Viktor was considered rehabilitated and released and through the intervention of human rights activists in the United States and in Israel, after years more of struggling to eke out a living tutoring in the Russian countryside, he was eventually allowed to secure a visa to leave the country. Being Jewish, he went first to live in Israel, where he remained for five years. His dream, however, was to live and teach in the United States of America. He was finally able to do so when he was granted political asylum. He had hopes of soon becoming a naturalized citizen, swearing his allegiance to his new country. With his credentials he had hoped for a teaching position at a university such as Harvard or Brown, or some other such prestigious Ivy League institution of higher learning. But no such offer was ever made. Not even from a state university. Or a community college. He had had numerous interviews but no offers of employment ever materialized. He didn't realize it, but the problem lay in the fact that, try as he might, his command of the English Language was so poor, his accent so heavy, most folks could not understand much of what he said. And this, finally, is what brought him to Orel Robarts Bible College of the Ozarks. No one here cared if he could be understood or not. In fact, the administration preferred that no one could understand his lectures. He was, after all, an esteemed foreign author and poet. He had some reputation in the literary world and he had published widely, mostly books of poems that no one had ever read, as well as a book of essays on Russian literature. In other words, he had a resume loaded with achievement. And he could not be understood in normal conversation. This made him ideal for Robarts, since he would be teaching courses the college didn't particularly want understood to begin with. After an initial interview in which no one on the interviewing committee had the slightest notion what he had said in response to their searching questions, Viktor was hired on the spot. He happily accepted, thinking that this would be, however meager, at least a starting point from which to build his new career teaching at the college level in America. Who could tell where it all might lead? This was America after all, the land of opportunity.

So Viktor made his way to class. The students, polite as ever, were patiently and anxiously waiting for him when he arrived, sweating and flustered. Fourteen shiny young Bible students, all remarkably white and entirely protestant, waiting quietly, in their fundamentalist sort of way, some reading to themselves from the Good Book, others just staring out the window, nervously waiting for the man they thought they were supposed to admire but could barely understand.

"Greedings, students," Viktor said, "A lasht, I am ere."

"What did he say?" one girl whispered to the girl sitting next to her. She shook her head. "Something about bleating something. Not sure what that means."

Murmurs drifted about the classroom as everyone was waiting for Professor Karshenko to pass out the exam. They would have two hours to explain the intricacies of *War and Peace*, and other classics of Russian literature. None of them had actually read *War and Peace*, or any of the other works that had been assigned over the semester, but some had seen the movie and a few had read the Classics Comic book, and some even had purchased the Cliffnotes or gone on-line, so most of them at least knew the general idea hidden within Tolstoy's masterpiece. They were certain that that would be enough. Also they were aware that Professor Karshenko could not read English much better than he could speak it in conversation. Sometimes he read out loud to the class in English and sometimes, just to amuse himself and revel in the rich tones of the Mother Tongue, he read in Russian, a language none of the students spoke or understood. It made no particular difference. It all sounded the same to the students. As a result, he was very generous when it came to grades. No one ever failed. And, of course, no one was ever sent to Siberia. It could be a lonely life for an aging Jew from Odessa, however. A lonely life, indeed.

But there was one bright spot developing for Viktor already that day. That morning's mail had brought a confirmation of his new contract with God+Write, the summer writing conference to be held out in Oregon. He wasn't entirely sure where Oregon was exactly, but he was pleased to have the opportunity to visit other parts of the United States, particularly the old west, and to get paid for it at the same time. He had seen some of the early western movies, with John Wayne and Gary Cooper, and had some idea what he might expect to find in the rugged bad lands of the Western United States. The proffered stipend was not great, but it was enough to supplement his salary at Robarts, which also wasn't great, and if offered expenses as well, including airfare and room and board at the conference, which was held up at a lake, Wallowa Lake, at a campground high in the mountains. He understood that he would be teaching workshops in poetry and essay writing to adult students of all ages who wanted to be Christian writers. He would also be giving readings for the participants and for the general public. It struck him as odd that they would want a Jew for what was billed as a Christian writing conference, but they seemed impressed with his credentials, and particularly, for some strange reason, the fact that he had received an honor known as the Noble Prize. He had not been aware that the prize held much interest outside of Lubbock, Texas, where the prize committee of the South Lubbock Evangelical Council had chosen to honor him for his writing. The prize had been named after one of the Council's chief benefactors, Julia Noble, the ex-wife of a Texas oil baron, T. Gaither Noble, who had funded the annual award of one thousand dollars. But Viktor had listed the award on his resume when he responded to their ad in the classified section of the monthly magazine, *The Writing Life*, and they had seemed to be impressed. As a result, he had been told by God+Write that he would be considered the "Big Name" writer at the conference, the star attraction. He couldn't have been more pleased. It never occurred to him that the Board of Directors of the God+Write conference might have mistakenly thought he had actually won the Nobel Prize for Literature, with its award of one million dollars. While none of them actually knew what winning that prize entailed, they harbored some hope, if not an expectation, that such a nest egg sitting idly by awaiting Viktor's retirement, might spur him to want to share some of it with the conference, a non-profit corporation, in some generous way and might perhaps fund the expansion of the conference into year-around offerings with an endowment of some size. But it should be acknowledged that small religious colleges and organizations tend to make such mistakes rather easily. And occasionally, they strike it rich.

Yes, the summer was shaping up to be an enjoyable one. As soon as these exams had been completed, graded and the grades turned in, Viktor decided he would need to be off to the local Walmart to find an inexpensive pair of boots and a small backpack. He had been told they would be essential for life in the wilderness of northeastern Oregon. Little did he know how true that was going to be.

CHAPTER 9

CANDI HAD SEEN THE ANNOUNCEMENT UP ON THE BULLETIN BOARD IN the student lounge. It read, "GOD+WRITE SUMMER CHRISTIAN WRITING CONFERENCE, Wallowa Lake, Oregon, July 15th through July 31st. Distinguished faculty of Christian poets and writers, including Viktor Karshenko, recipient of the Nobel Prize for Literature. Workshops, inspirational readings, social gatherings in an atmosphere of Christian love and caring. Renew your connection with the Spirit of God and your own path to creativity in one of God's most scenic settings. See Professor Kees, Dept. of English and Literature for details. A limited number of scholarships are available."

Candi read the announcement over several times. Her eyes focused on the possibility of a scholarship. It would be a chance to get away from the city and the strip club for two whole weeks in the middle of the summer and she would have the opportunity to return to such a wonderful place, a place she had visited each summer of her teenage years, and knew so well, when she attended church camp there. It was too much for her to resist. She immediately headed for Professor Kees' office. She knocked at the door.

"Come in."

She entered to find Professor Kees sitting at his desk in his tiny office, his feet propped up on the side bar. He was in shirtsleeves, his sport coat hanging carelessly over the back of his shabby and tilting executive chair. He was busy correcting examination papers, a tall stack of them on the desk at his side. His feet thumped to the floor, as he quickly stood up when she came in.

"Candice, er, Ms Summers. What can I do for you?" Kees sat back down and directed her toward one of the side chairs in front of his desk, quickly positioning himself to get the best view of her as possible, without being too overt about it. "I'm very involved at the moment." He pointed to the stack of exam papers.

"Yes, I know," said Candi, as she sat down and instinctively crossed her legs in a slightly seductive maneuver. "I won't keep you. But I just read the announcement on the bulletin board about the God+Write Christian Writing Conference at Wallowa Lake and wondered if you would have time to give me some more information about it. I'd love to go." She paused, and then said quietly, "Money is a problem for me, however, and I was wondering about the scholarships that are said to be available. If there are any still not taken, I would like to apply for one."

Kees nodded, as he stared furtively at her legs and took in the fact that her short skirt had worked its way up her thighs.

"I'll give you the forms and you can complete them and return them to me as quickly as possible. The deadline is this coming Friday." He paused, bending down over his file cabinet. "We have had a number of interested students who have filled out applications already, but I'm sure the committee will give you full consideration." He plucked a packet of forms from one of the files and handed it to her. He smiled his best professorial smile. "I can certainly give you a good recommendation."

"Oh, I'd be so grateful if you could."

Candi slowly uncrossed her legs, stood up and thanked him. Without thinking, she gave him her best stripper, lap-dancer smile, took the packet of forms that Professor Kees held out to her, moved toward the door and eased her way out of the office, wiggling her backside slightly as she left, a subtle bump and grind. It did not go unnoticed by the good professor.

After she had gone only a faint whiff of her perfume remained to leave him slightly intoxicated. He sat back down at his desk and, for a brief moment, gazed soulfully out the window at the heavy traffic sliding past the campus on the freeway, the late afternoon sun glittering off the hoods of commuter cars heading home. He thought briefly of poor old Lucy, off to Mt. Vernon. But summer may just be looking even better, he mused, as he turned back to the work at hand. Or Summers, as the case may be. It was difficult to return to the boring exams on his desk. Visions of Ms Summers twitching and wiggling her way out of the office lingered in his thoughts, along with the last traces of her perfume, as he once again waded into the array of multiple choice questions and answers. True or false? True or false? A,B,C,or D? None of the above. So far George W. Bush was winning the poetry wars. Russell had been feeling a bit down as a result. But now that had all suddenly changed. After all, the prospects of darling Lucy stuck with her aging parents in Mt. Vernon and he in the Wallowas enjoying the pleasures of God+Write as well as, quite possibly, Ms. Summers, was enough to make him smile to himself. He stared at the ceiling. He would have to write an especially compelling recommendation for this remarkable student, he thought. One of the best he had ever had the pleasure of teaching. Inspired, he set aside the exam papers and turned to his computer and began immediately composing his letter of recommendation. Normally it was a duty he despised. But not this time. Yes, he concluded with a flourish, she was perhaps the very finest student he had ever had the pleasure of having in class, one who was always head and shoulders above the rest. One who set the bar incredibly high. A credit to East Hills Liberty College. He could recommend her without reservation. God+Write could only benefit spiritually and intellectually from her presence at the conference. Souls would someday be brought to Jesus with the talents she displayed. (He was sure this last comment would score lots of points even if nothing else did.) Visions of Candi's exit from his office lingered lovingly as he sniffed the air for traces of her perfume and turned back to the more serious, but less intriguing, business of George W. Bush and the wonders of the world of poetry.

CHAPTER 10

CANDI SPENT THE WEEK STUDYING FOR AND TAKING EXAMS, AS WELL AS filling out the forms for the scholarship application to the God + Write conference. It included a requirement for a three-page essay on why God had called her to be a Christian writer. She struggled a bit with that, but by Friday the exams were over, and the forms and the essay had been completed and submitted to Professor Kees. He had seemed delighted to see her and assured her that her application would receive his personal attention and that he had written a strong letter of recommendation on her behalf to the scholarship committee. It would not hurt that he was a member of that committee.

She was confident that she had done well on her exams but was still apprehensive about the scholarship application. She feared that her essay had not adequately conveyed her deep feelings of faith and her trust in the Lord. But the more she thought about getting away from the city and the strip club for part of the summer, and especially returning to the Wallowa Mountains, the more it intrigued and excited her. Not since her summers at the church camp had she been back. Despite some misgivings about her encounters there with Pastor Bob, she had come to love and even romanticize her memories of that scenic area. In her mind's eye she could still see the high mountains set against the intense blue sky of summer. The lake spread out like dark velvet, rippling in the sunlight. The sleepy little cow-town of Joseph that lay at the northern end of the lake. The campgrounds, lodge and recreational facilities that took up the southern end. The terminal moraine that stretched itself along the eastern rim of the lake, brown and treeless. She could remember visiting the gravesites and the monument to Old Chief Joseph, leader of the Nez Perce tribe, which overlooked the lake and kept its constant vigil. This was Nez Perce country, after all, a land and a history soaked with the blood of its people.

But suddenly her reverie was interrupted by the realization that she had to get to work. Gordie would be on her case if she were late again. Yes, another night at the strip club. Nockers' Up-Town Bar and Grille was crowded when she arrived for work that Friday evening. It had been a hot day and Candi was already drenched in sweat as she stripped down to her working clothes, a pair of thong panties and a skimpy bra. The club had no air-conditioning. Gordon Nockers had been promising for months to get it installed, but never wanted to put out the money for it. His little office at the back had a window air-conditioner in it, and he was comfortable even if no one else was. Big Cal watched her as she disrobed. He felt it was always his private performance. She caught him staring, and smiled at him and winked. He quickly looked away, embarrassed and red-faced. Poor Cal, she thought, as she looked into the mirror and applied some last minute make-up to her cheeks. She always felt better knowing that he was there.

"Well, time to get it on," she said to him as she passed by him and left the confines of the back room. She was the first dancer of the evening and the boys were getting antsy waiting for the action to begin. She could hear the low hum of conversation, the click of pool balls from the far corner pool tables, the clanking of glasses, the TV blaring out the latest sports scores. Then suddenly the place went quiet with anticipation. The TV went dead. The pool games ceased and the faces of the men glowed with perspiration and expectation. The spotlights hit her as she stepped out onto the runway built above and behind the bar, and she immediately began to gyrate around the shiny metal pole that reached to the ceiling, the background music now at full volume for her entrance and the crowd cheering her on. Despite her misgivings about the work, she had to admit that it gave her a rush when she first stepped into the lights. Show Biz. She had clearly become one of the favorites of the house and all of her regulars were there, especially the cops, bunched around the stage area, yelling and waving, and cheering her on. Slowly and seductively she slid herself up and down the pole, wrapping her legs around it, pulling herself up and up, simulating sexual excitement as she went. The men beneath her were pounding their beer bottles and drink glasses on the bar in time to the music, spurring her on. She could see their faces grinning up at her as she twirled around and around. All in a day's work, she thought, as she casually simulated masturbation. They really loved that move. She could see Cal at the back of the lounge keeping watch over the crowd for any disturbance. Keeping watch over his secret girl, Candi.

And then she saw Jesse. He had slipped in and was standing several feet inside the entrance. She could see that he was watching her intently. She tried not to let him know that she had seen him. He drifted along the back wall to an empty table, sat down and Sylvie, one of the cocktail waitresses, immediately took his order for a beer. He drank slowly as Candi continued to dance, never taking his eyes off her. She'd better make sure Cal knew he was there, she thought, in case he makes any trouble. He had called her a number of times but this was the first time she had seen him since the breakup. The music built to a thunderous climax as she tried her best to do the same, writhing in a fit of feigned ecstasy. The music stopped and the place went silent for a brief moment, then broke into loud applause as the men expressed their appreciation for her efforts. She skipped down the runway stairs to the barroom floor and waltzed her way among the men gathered around, collecting money as she went, letting them stuff bills into her bra and panties. It was not something she really cared to do, but it was all part of the act, and that's when the money rolled in. That, and from the private lap dances in the other room. Their fingers, groped at her flesh, their nails, often dirty and ragged from a day's hard physical work, sometimes dug into her. But she flashed her best pole dancer's smile and knew that soon one of the patrons would beckon her over for a private dance performance, the music would start up again, and the money would continue to roll In. The power of fantasy.

And it worked. Soon one of the boys, a guy she hadn't seen before, motioned her over, offered her his lap and the music blared forth again. Candi climbed aboard and off she went, whirling around and around, pushing her breasts into the sweating face before her as he lay back, moaning quietly, and let her body churn back and forth over his now bulging crotch. Candi looked up at the strobe lights and just let her mind drift off, back to her memories of Wallowa Lake, the cooling waters of that lake so deep it had been said no one ever drowned there, since their bodies were never found. They just went down and down forever. A lake so clear and pristine no one would ever be unclean again who had soaked in its waters. She needed that.

From the back of the room Jesse, already slightly red from a little crank earlier in the evening, watched with a mixture of fascination and disgust. This woman, this girl, who had been his, with whom he had shared a bed, was now rotating around and around on some asshole's lap, some shitheel who was stuffing bills in her clothing. Who did she think she was to be rejecting him when she was willing to ride some guy's dick for a buck? He finished his beer and stumbled out of the club, slamming the door behind him. No one but Cal seemed to notice. Candi looked down at her benefactor and smiled her most expensive smile. He sighed and grinned, pushed another bill into her bra, and the ride was over.

When she looked up, she was thankful to see that Jesse was gone.

CHAPTER 11

CANDI HAD NOT BEEN AWARE OF HIS PRESENCE, BUT PROFESSOR KEES was also in the club that night, and had watched her dance performance with both surprise and amazement, as well as great interest. The good professor had sat half-hidden behind one of the pillars that acted as supports for the ceiling, far back in the shadows of the smoky barroom, his face aglow with the wonders of her athletic movements, her energy, her tight, young body, twisting, turning, moving back and forth across the lit runway. He was mesmerized, as he absentmindedly sipped his beer and pondered the wonders of her scholarship application to the God+Write Christian Writing Conference. There must be a God after all, he thought.

Candi, his star pupil, had not mentioned her work here at the strip club on her application form. He had been totally unaware of her weekend occupation. It had been purely, or impurely, by chance that with dear Lucy off to Mt. Vernon he had slipped out of the empty house looking for a cool refreshment and some diversion. Cruising slowly down McNary Avenue in the old Volvo stationwagon, he had been drawn by the flashing and colorful neon lights of the reader board in the parking lot of Nockers' Up-Town Bar and Grille, promising 'GIRLS! GIRLS! and more GIRLS!, Dancing for the Entertainment and Pleasure of Gentlemen Exclusively! XXX Rated!" he was hooked. The Play Boy Club it wasn't, but Nockers' would be good enough to possibly salve a lonely guy's needs. And here, unexpectedly, was his very favorite student. And dancing her heart out too. She was all the more his favorite now. He stared at her, seeing her now in a new light, admiring her moves. Her exotic smiles. Only hours before he had been grading her examination paper, oblivious to the full extent of her talents. Despite the fact that she too thought that George W. Bush might have written the line of poetry quoted in the exam, he realized now that she clearly had talents that had formerly been somewhat undercover in the classroom. They were now more fully revealed. Clearly she was passing this course with flying colors.

He sat quietly out of sight while she moved through the crowd gathering up her rewards, then he quickly and quietly slipped out of the club before she could get to where he was seated. He felt, somehow, it would be better if they did not meet in this way. He did not want to embarrass either her or himself.

He walked out into the parking lot, climbed into the old Volvo stationwagon and drove slowly down the street toward home. The empty old house wouldn't seem quite so empty tonight. That night, erotic dreams of Candi and the possibilities of the God+Write Conference danced through his dreams. He hadn't had a wet dream in years. To hell with George W. Bush, he thought. He knew an A student when he saw one. And tonight, he had certainly seen one.

CHAPTER 12

VIKTOR KNELT DOWN TO RETIE THE LACES OF HIS NEW HIKING BOOTS. He had bought them for a bargain price at Walmart, along with a sturdy looking backpack. The boots had been made in El Salvador, and the backpack in Tibet. The boots were new and stiff and his feet were already sore. Wearing the heavy socks, made in China, which he also had been advised by the store clerk to buy, made the boots a little too snug and he could feel the blisters beginning to form on his big toes. To make matters worse, he had loaded up his new backpack with large rocks from his garden to test it out, and to get accustomed to toting a heavy load on his back, and the rocks kept shifting from side to side as he walked or bent over, throwing him off balance. This business of hiking might not be as much fun as he had imagined, he thought, as he continually tried to maintain himself on the rough path. He was convinced he needed to break in his new gear and also to begin improving his conditioning. It had been a long time since he had had to physically exert himself to any great extent. He wanted to be prepared for the wilds of eastern Oregon. Not since his years in Siberia had Viktor needed to walk long distances on difficult and hilly terrains, especially on an unpaved surface. A short jaunt into the foothills of the Ozarks would surely be just the sort of preparation he would need. Ever since, in an effort to improve his English, he had recently read a book by Reinhold Zuber, entitled *"The Power of the Moment,"* he had been looking forward to the idea of getting back to nature and immersing himself in what was happening at any given second of his life. That was the essential teaching of Zuber. Get back to nature and absorb the moment in all its glory. Where better to do that than here, hiking in the Ozarks? Zuber, better known to the academic world as an existential theologian and an expert on the works of fellow theologian, Paul Tillich, had unexpectedly struck pure gold with his study of the meaning of life through focusing entirely on the present moment, to the exclusion of the past or the future. It was an idea that somehow took off in the book world with sales in the millions following his appearance on the Oprah Winfrey show. Oprah had proclaimed it one of the great books of all time, a book that had remade her life, and it immediately reached number one on the New York Times Best Seller List. It stayed there for well over a year, and made Zuber a very wealthy man. He was able to retire and move to the Bahamas. An audio version was brought out, narrated by Clint Eastwood, making clever use of his Dirty Harry voice, and soon a film version, starring Tom Cruise, would be appearing in theaters all across the country. It had been rumored in the tabloids that Cruise was so taken with the concept of living entirely within the moment that he was seriously thinking of giving up his immersion in Scientology and becoming an avid follower of Zuber, now considered by many to be a genuine guru. Zuber was currently devoting all his waking hours to the lecture circuit, for which he received big bucks, and to the moment itself, the true revelation of becoming, and now he was even looking for ways to be in the moment when asleep. Paul Tillich rapidly receded into the past. A sequel, *The Power of the Nano-moment*, was already in the anxious hands of his publisher.

The invitation to Viktor to be the star member of the faculty at the God+Write Christian Writing Conference in the Wallowa Mountains had coincided with his new found interest in "The Moment," and Viktor saw his new philosophy as truly a gift from the Almighty, although he had to admit, he had never been a great fan of the Almighty before. But now he reveled in this opportunity to commune with nature and with God and to seize the power of the moment at the same time. At this particular moment, however, his feet hurt. His back was sore. The backpack was ill-fitting and clumsy, and he wasn't sure he was really enjoying himself and the moment all that much.

The trail wound through lush, green woodlands and had a relatively gentle elevation gain that nonetheless taxed Viktor's stamina to the max, leaving him winded and gasping for breath. As an academic, he was no longer accustomed to this sort of physical exertion. But still, he had almost a month to build himself up before his sojourn into the high mountains of the Wallowa country, and he was certain he could do so. After all, he had survived Siberia, the aftermath of the Stalin years, and the KGB. This should be a snap compared with all that. He had now hiked, however, for the better part of an hour. He was exhausted. A sudden pain in his chest caused him to quickly reach in his pocket for his nitro tablets. He put one under his tongue and took a swig of water from his new canteen (made in Malaysia). The pain subsided as quickly as it had come. He looked around. He was no longer even certain where he was. He took out his new compass (made in Japan) and opened it hesitantly. He had never used a compass before, but the salesman at Walmart had said that every mountaineer should carry one at all times for just such occasions. There were no instructions with it. Ah, he thought, gazing at the dial. That must be north. The needle had jumped, swinging wildly, and then it settled down. But, so what? he asked himself. He was puzzled. Perhaps he was lost. He wasn't sure. It seemed that unless he knew where he was going and how he was to get there, it didn't matter very much which way was north.

The trail had divided into two and then divided again. He could try to retrace his steps and follow it back but wasn't sure which fork to take to get back home. He closed the compass case and put it back in the pocket of the new REI trousers (made in Columbia) he had bought, the ones with the zippered legs that could be made into shorts. Slowly, and with a pained look on his face, he tried to retrace his steps. His feet ached more and more. His blistered toes felt the size of walnuts. The backpack dug into his sides and back, sliding from side to side, rubbing the skin raw. The significance of the power of the moment was beginning to escape him. What does it matter, he wondered, if the meaning of the moment is to be simply lost? "Whose woods these are I think I know," a line from Frost crept into his mind, as he surveyed the scene. But Frost was no help at all. And where was Zuber when he needed something more than the power of the moment. As Viktor tramped on his thoughts were now entirely concentrated on the pain in his lower back, the straps digging into his shoulders, and his aching feet, the growing blisters, and the trail that seemed to be wandering off into unfamiliar territory. Zuber was rapidly being replaced by the immediate reality of the moment. Perhaps for a true intellectual like himself the answers to the questions of existence really did lie in the works of Paul Tillich, after all. "In such suffering do we truly live."

CHAPTER 13

REDD BENSON, EXECUTIVE DIRECTOR OF THE GOD+WRITE CHRISTIAN Writing Conference, settled back in the wooden rocking chair that served as his desk chair and reviewed the registration forms that had been arriving and were now piling up from all over the country, as well as a few foreign countries, along with the coveted enclosed checks, which he was most gratified to see. His given name was actually Reddick, but since childhood he had always been known simply as "Redd," with two ds. Since he did not have red hair, but rather a bushy thatch of curly black hair, this shortening of his name always confused those who had just met him for the first time. He liked it that way.

It was late in June and the conference was set to begin in only a few more weeks. Redd had numerous loose ends to tie together before then. The campground had been cleared of trash, the cabins and yurts had been cleaned out, and repairs had been made where needed. There had been a Boy Scout Jamboree held at the campground over the past week, and the place had been a mess. Removing the dead, decomposed remains of a skunk from beneath the floorboards of the shower stalls in the main building had not been easy, and the smell still lingered. But all in all, everything was almost ready for occupancy, including the private cabins by the lake that had been rented and especially reserved for the staff and guest instructors.

Benson was a defrocked minister from Idaho. He had run afoul of some of his denomination's ethics rules (which were not too many to begin with) and he had been ousted a number of years earlier. The Third Church of Christ the Savior, an ultra-conservative denomination based in southern Oregon, had been unable to accommodate his ongoing interest in child pornography. When he posted an ad on Craig's List trolling for nude photo exchanges with young boys, using the church's office computer, and later personally showing up at a house in Boise, Idaho that had, unbeknownst to him, been rented by CBS television in an expose of pedophiles, a show that was broadcast nationally time and time again, leading to his arrest and subsequent plea of "nolo contendere," the church fathers concluded they had had enough of Redd Benson. He was cut loose from his position. His mail order degree and subsequent ordination were revoked, and he was shunned by the members of the church.

After his probation was completed, in disgrace he bummed around the country for a couple of years, working odd jobs, trying to get another foothold on the gravy train. Eventually he found himself in the great State of Texas, in the heart of the Bible belt. There, he found work with the Jesus Saves Broadcasting System - known simply as JSBS - out of Corpus Christi, where he soon discovered there was a great deal of money to be made in bringing men's souls to Jesus through television evangelism. Redd started as a lowly prop man for a show called "Soul Power," with the Reverend Dr. Billy Bussy and his wife, a bleached blonde ex-casino card dealer named Mindy, known primarily for her outrageous make-up, her ability to cry on cue (causing mascara to run in thick, dark rivers down her cheeks), a white poodle dog named Joshua, and her pink Mercedes convertible. The job paid only minimum wage, which in Texas wasn't much, but it was the start of his rehabilitation and his introduction to the lucrative world of televised religion, with all its potentials for tax dodges and off-shore money laundering.

Over the next two years Redd worked his way into the minds, hearts and pocket books of several of the sponsors of Soul Power and soon was being primed for a show of his own, "Do Unto

Others." The premise of the production was that anyone, however uneducated, stupid or poor, could be rich if he or she just gave enough money, hopefully on a regular basis and with automatic bank withdrawals, to "Pastor" Redd. The show was a great success especially among the elderly poor living in rundown trailer parks across America, all close to death and feeling an intense need for a spiritual insurance policy. Pastor Redd provided it. Eventually, however, the show and Pastor Redd found themselves being investigated by the IRS, a result of their failure to get enough of their own kind elected to national office, although Texas had done more than its share in that regard, and Pastor Redd, facing time in the Big Slam for tax evasion, given his prior record, had his attorney work out a plea bargain whereby he would discontinue the scam, pay a hefty fine, plus back taxes, and he could escape a prison term. He gladly accepted the government's plea bargain.

So that is how it was that Redd Benson, no longer known as "Pastor Redd," came to become the executive director of God+Write, the annual Christian Writing Conference. With nowhere else to go, following his crash and burn in Texas, he returned to his home territory in the Pacific Northwest. He was hired by God+Write Christian Writing Conference primarily because no one else with any credentials wanted the job, so far removed as it was from any real population center or pot of easy gold. In the world of evangelism, God+Write was considered small time. In a sense, he felt had descended to this. It was rather like ending up in purgatory, and he accepted his fate. The salary was minimal and the accommodations were small and undistinguished. This was certainly not what he had been accustomed to with the television station. No highly polished, gold lacquered furniture with rich, burgundy upholstery. No plush carpeting. No dramatic altar or fake stone statues of angels. The conference was maintained mostly by modest grants from various evangelical religious organizations, and the registration and tuition fees paid by the participants themselves. There was an abbreviated winter conference in February and the main show in July. In between God+Write sponsored workshops in various churches throughout the region, mostly in rural areas of the Pacific Northwest. Over the past five years of its existence, God+Write Christian Writing Conference had gained a national following of novice Christian writers anxious to break into the supposedly lucrative field of Christian literature. At least that was how the opportunities were presented in the ads that ran in various religious magazines on sale at the Christian supply stores. "EASY MONEY DOING GOD'S WORK RIGHT FROM THE COMFORT OF YOUR OWN HOME! BE A CHRISTIAN WRITER!"

Redd's small office in Joseph, some six miles from the conference grounds by the lake, was quiet and the town a peaceful place, an odd mixture of cowboys and artists, as well as fugitives from large cities seeking to be as far from civilization as it was humanly possible to be. This was the perfect setting for the former evangelical pastor to lick his wounds and kick start his career. After all of the negative publicity over the pedophile expose and the close call with the IRS that had wiped him out financially, he was finally ready for a more relaxed and secluded life.

CHAPTER 14

JESSE'S BIRTH CERTIFICATE LISTED HIS NAME AS JESSE IRWIN ZAFARELLI. His father, Gino, a first generation child of Italian immigrants, had operated a produce stand at the farmers' market in the Old Italian neighborhood of lower Southeast Portland for many years. His mother, Helena, had been a stay-at-home mom. She was said to have been a descendent of French-Canadian fur trappers. Her great-great grandfather had come to the Oregon Territory in the mid 1800s from Quebec. Jesse didn't mind his name, Zafarelli, until he was in the upper grades of elementary school when the other boys realized his initials spelled out the word "jiz" and they began to make fun of him constantly. "Here comes jiz!" they'd yell out on the playground or in the school cafeteria, grabbing their crotches and pretending to squirt their dicks at him whenever he approached one of them. "Here cums Jiz" would sometimes be written on the classroom blackboard when he arrived at home room. Jesse would quickly erase the board, his face burning with embarrassment. It wasn't until he was big enough and strong enough to do some damage to some of them that the taunting finally stopped. For the most part, anyway. Every now and then, however, he would run into an old classmate, and that was always what they remembered about him. He was Jiz.

Finally, about a year ago, while he was doing six months on his second DUI at the Multnomah County Minimum Security Correctional Facility in East Multnomah County, Jesse met Jimmy Eagle Feather, who occupied the upper bunk in the minimum security dormitory. Jimmy claimed to be an enrolled member of the Blackfeet tribe from Montana. Jimmy did his best to look and act the part and at first his activities annoyed the piss out of Jesse, thumping on the frame of the metal bunk bed, moaning in strange sounds and making rhythms in the middle of the night, talking all the time about the "Great Spirit".

But it wasn't long before Jesse discovered something about himself through Jimmy. Jesse happened to mention once that his mother was descended from French-Canadian fur trapper stock. Jimmy immediately informed him that all those horny fur trappers and traders mixed with the Indian women, there being no white women available in the early territorial days, and that Jesse himself likely had Native American blood coursing through his veins. Jesse had never thought about this before. But suddenly it clicked in his head. In his need to be someone, it made sense to him. He must be an Indian.

Soon he had grown his dark, wavy hair long and began to pull it back into a ponytail. He, later, even had his arms tattooed with primitive-looking designs taken from photos of stone petroglyphs he found in a National Geographic magazine in the prison library. He began to emulate Jimmy's ceremonial moaning and drumming, much to the chagrin of the other inmates in their dormitory. And he even found and actually read, slowly however, a book on Indian tribes of the Northwest and their origins and customs, something he had not done since he had dropped out of high school ten years ago. He decided, given the various places where his mother's family had lived in the old days, that he must be Nez Perce. Finally, with a great show of bravado, he changed his name to Jesse Red Hawk. He didn't do this legally in court, of course. But to everyone he knew and met, he became Jesse Red Hawk. Finally he had an identity that brought him some sense of pride and community. Something he felt he had never had before. When he first met Candi at the strip club she had remarked on his odd dress and his long hair. She had found him interesting and appealing in a primitive sort of way.

He was the first Italian-Indian she had ever known. Of course, once she got to know Jesse and had thrown him out of the apartment, it no longer mattered to her.

Still he thought of himself as Native American. "Zafarelli" was a thing of the past. His parents had no idea what had gotten into him. His mother insisted she had no idea whether or not there was Indian blood in the family history. His mother's maiden name had been French, "La Tour." Certainly, it was a possibility there could have been an Indian in the mix somewhere, but that was all it was, a mere possibility. But that was good enough for Jesse. He was now "Red Hawk," a brave warrior. He started traveling around the Northwest Indian circuit attending Indian Pow Wows with Jimmy Eagle Feather and trying to learn more sophisticated dances and drumming techniques.

So, as he sat alone night after night in his room at the Double Six motel, Indian as he was, he still felt disconnected from himself and his past. He often thought of Candi. He had heard through the grapevine that she was hoping to go to some writing conference at Wallowa Lake, his old ancestral lands. He should be there too, he thought. He knew of the town of Joseph and that the Nez Perce tribe was going to celebrate the annual Chief Joseph Days in late July. He'd read that in "Appaloosa News," the more or less monthly newsletter now edited by Jimmy Eagle Feather. Perhaps, Jesse mused, he might even be a descendent of Chief Joseph himself. That noble warrior. One of the survivors of the epic battles of Big Hole and Bear Paw. If Candi knew that, maybe she'd come to realize her mistake and take him back. He decided, for these various reasons, he should return to the place of his spiritual beginnings, the land of his people. He looked around at the dingy motel room. Anything, he thought, to get out of this shithole.

CHAPTER 15

THE PARKING LOT WAS CROWDED WITH AN ASSORTMENT OF PICK-UP trucks, campers, junkers of various makes, and the occasional Plymouth station wagon, when Jesse again exited Nockers' Up-Town Bar and Grille and headed home to the motel. It had rained while he was in the club watching Candi again performing for the perverts. He got some odd thrill out of sitting in the shadows of the club watching her.

The sidewalks were slick and shiny beneath the glow of the streetlamps. Jesse was still on foot, as his truck had been impounded by the State authorities as a result of his probationary status with the court. It made it very difficult to maintain a decent sex life without access to wheels. But now he was not in such a good mood. Being both on foot and having just seen his ex-girl friend taking off her clothes for a bar full of assholes had done nothing for his outlook on life.

After a quick stop at an all night convenience store to pick up another six-pack of Bud and a couple of corndogs, Jesse made his way home to the Double Six. His life, which had never been that great to begin with, had really turned to shit on him lately. First six months in the county slam with Jimmy Eagle Feather; then the second drunk driving conviction and the loss of his truck, and now Candi dumping him. He tried to tell himself that he had dumped her; but deep down, he knew that wasn't so. The porch light above his doorway had burned out. He wrestled with the key, while balancing the beer and the corndogs, and finally got the door open without spilling anything. He threw his baseball cap, the one with the Blitz logo on the front, across the room. He scored a hit when it landed perfectly on the back of a chair by the TV set. The first thing that had gone right so far today. Jesse lay down on the bed and consumed his corndogs, wiping the smears of mustard off his hands on the bedcover as well as quickly downing the first of the six-pack of beer.

He flicked the remote and the old TV burst into life. The late night news had just begun and local newscasters were tossing jokes and light banter back and forth amongst themselves, oblivious to their audience, trying vainly to transition from one inane feature story to another. There was what they called "breaking news," as the anchor quickly passed off to a reporter in the field, standing under a streetlamp on an undisclosed street corner somewhere in Southeast Portland, where a missing puppy had been found, much to the sobbing relief of its owner. Fortunately the dog was in good health, having been checked out pro bono by a local veterinarian, who was also interviewed at some length, and world order had once again been restored. "Back to you in the studio, Bryan," someone named Tracy announced glibly, as if she had just reported on the start of World War III. Jesse could not have cared less in either event.

He finished off the last scrap of corndog, picked his teeth momentarily with one of the pointed sticks and then tossed the sticks at the wastebasket in the far corner on the other side of the room, hoping to continue his hot streak and score some more points, but he missed. Except for the glow of the television screen, the room lay in darkness. He got up and closed the drapes. He needed a woman, he thought. Bad! Really bad! Immediately his thoughts turned back to Candi. Visions of her dancing in front of all the other men, their eyes eating her up, their hands reaching for her, passed through his befuddled mind. He reached for another beer.

"Shit," he yelled at the TV, and switched to a channel where some washed up soap opera actor was peddling a concoction guaranteed to increase penis size. "Shit," Jesse yelled again. Someone in the room above him thumped on the floor in protest. He ignored it. When would Candi wake up and realize that college was just so much bullshit, her job at the club was just so much bullshit, and would come back to him, begging for it? He thought of calling her again, but realized she would not be home from the club yet, and that she always turned off her cell phone when she was at work. He stood up, removed his work boots, dropped his jeans to the floor, took off his denim shirt, pulled the bedcover back and sat on the edge of the bed. The time would come, he thought. The time would come when she would need him. Whenever that was, he knew he'd best be ready. Jesse Red Hawk, the Italian Nez Perce extraordinaire would come to the rescue.

On the television a group of bleached blonde young bimbos in mini-skirts up to their navels were sitting around in a circle extolling the virtues and pleasures of E-Z-Xtend, the wonder supplement. All their boyfriends used it, they claimed. Jesse pulled down his tattered shorts and closely examined his own penis. "It's been awhile since you've been seen any action, Big Guy," he said out loud. And then he puffed up with satisfaction as he quickly made some mental measurements. Those gals hadn't seen anything. Then he pulled up his underwear and flicked off the TV. The room disappeared into complete darkness. The night closed in around him. It was good to be Indian, he thought, but at least some part of him was still Italian. Maybe the best part. Ah, Jesse Red Hawk, The Italian Stallion.

CHAPTER 16

CANDI HAD BEEN WAITING PATIENTLY FOR DAYS, BOTH FOR HER GRADES from her final exams, and for a response to her application for a scholarship to the God+Write Christian Writing Conference. Both arrived on the same day, very early in July. She had been working late at the club that night and got home tired and out of sorts. The crowds that evening had been particularly obnoxious. But two long envelopes were tucked into her mailbox waiting for her. She tore open the envelope from the college first, and found that she had passed all of her courses and now had an accumulated grade point average of 3.87 for the spring term. She had even gotten an A from her literature class with Professor Kees. She had not expected that. She had not felt certain that she had done well on the final. Thinking back on the test questions, she was fairly certain George W. Bush had not written any poetry, let alone the quote given in the test.

Then she hesitantly tore open the envelope with the Joseph, Oregon return address, the one from God+Write, Inc. "Dear Miss Summers," it began, "We here at the God+Write Christian Writing Conference, in the spirit of our Savior, are pleased to inform you that your application for a scholarship to the God+Write Christian Writing Conference has been approved by the scholarship committee. This scholarship covers room and board as well as tuition. The conference commences on the 15th of July and concludes on the 31st of July. You will be responsible for your own personal, out of pocket expenses, as well as transportation to and from the conference site at Wallowa Lake. We welcome you to the conference and trust you will find it a rewarding experience and that it will make a fine contribution to your evolving spiritual life, preparing you for an exciting and lucrative career as a Christian writer. Please notify us immediately of your acceptance. Yours in Christ, our Lord," It was signed by Reddick Benson, Executive Director. There was a hand-drawn smiley face under his signature. Enclosed with the letter was a brochure outlining the specifics of the conference, including how to get a reservation on the bus that had been chartered to transport the conferees from the Portland area east to Wallowa Lake and back again, as well as information on alternative housing and the suggested materials that might be needed, as well as proper clothing.

Candi was thrilled. She immediately called her parents, despite the late hour. Then she called the club to talk with Gordie to arrange the time off from work. She had previously mentioned to Gordie the possibility that she might be attending the conference. He was not too pleased with the news, as the summer months were an especially busy time at the club. There were lots of conventions being held during that time of the year and the club would be packed with excited and horny conventioneers whooping and hollering and having a good, drunken time. He wanted his best girls there to entertain them. Gordie was already nursing a particularly bad migraine when Candi got through to him on the phone. He groaned audibly when she told him the good news. But as a good Christian himself he could hardly deny her the time off. "No work, no pay," he cautioned her, however.

I might actually become a great writer, Candi thought, as she reviewed the list of instructors and workshops that were being offered at the conference. She had to let them know soon which ones she would be taking, and she would need to send in some samples of her writing. She noticed that Professor Kees was among the instructors, and that he would be teaching a poetry workshop. She had never written any poetry, at least nothing she had ever shown to anyone, but she thought this might be just the opportunity to spread her wings and release some of the pent up emotions she had kept suppressed for so long. Poetry just might be the answer. As well as Professor Kees. He was always so nice to her. And he had given her an A for the spring term.

But what really excited her the most was the name of Viktor Karshenko, reported to have been a recipient of the Nobel Prize in Literature. She had never actually heard of him before, but neither had she ever been so close to anyone of that fame and reputation. She had never read anything he had written, but she was certain his greatness could rub off on her as it would on all the conferees. She could hardly wait. That the conference was taking place at Wallowa Lake, at her former church campground, a place she had known so well, was an added enducement.

Candi had a little less than two weeks to prepare. She would buy some new clothes, get some hiking gear, a backpack, proper hiking boots, and, of course, make sure her laptop was in top working order. She even decided she ought to call Jesse and give him the "good news," leaving a long, detailed message for him with the front desk clerk at the Double Six Motel. She knew her news would piss him off good. That'll take the brine out of his corned beef, she thought, her sense of Christian charity momentarily overcome with emotion.

CHAPTER 17

As THE BUS, AN AGING YELLOW SCHOOL BUS THAT HAD BEEN RENTED from a rental fleet, rolled into the campground at the south end of Wallowa Lake, Candi was excited to see again the familiar setting. It was late afternoon. Already the sun had dropped behind the mountains to the west, casting long shadows through the tall firs and pine trees that surrounded the lake, and there was a chill in the air despite the fact that it was the middle of July. The trip from Portland had been long and tiring, made longer by the stiffness of the bus springs, which seemed to capture every pothole and rough spot in the road. The conferees had bumped and rattled their way through the Columbia River Gorge, through The Dalles, away from the wide Columbia River, on into eastern Oregon to Pendleton, La Grande, and then, finally away from the I-84, northeast to Elgin, Wallowa, Lostine and then Joseph. And now, at last, the lake itself, deep in the far reaches of Wallowa County. It seemed like they were at the ends of the earth.

The lake was shimmering dark water as they cruised around the eastern shore beneath the dry, brown moraine that stretched the entire length of the lake. The Wallowas, like the Alps of Europe, rose stark against the darkening sky and, despite the summer season, there was snow on their peaks year around. Yes, it was still Nez Perce country, Candi thought, wild and beautiful. She could imagine, as she had done as a child, bands of Indians in their war paint on their horses careening down the sides of the foothills, whooping and ready for battle. Since she had been here last a tram system had been built that would take visitors up from the lake to the top of Mt. Howard, some 8,000 ft. high, to an alpine area of trails and viewpoints. She could see one of the small, silver gondolas swaying in the wind as it inched its way up the narrow clear cut on the mountain's side. A modern touch to the wilderness setting she thought. She was not sure that she approved.

The bus had been packed with passengers and their gear, duffel bags, suitcases, backpacks, and even a Kayak or two. Some of the passengers had arrived from other parts of the country and had been picked up at the Portland International Airport. One couple was from England. Others were from various parts of Western Canada and the United States. Most, however, were from Oregon or Washington, and most of them were from the Portland area or the upper Willamette Valley. Professor Kees was on board too. Candi had seen him sitting in the very back of the bus when she boarded in Oregon City, but she didn't get a chance to speak to him. She took a seat near the front and was soon conversing with a woman from southern Oregon who claimed to have been a missionary in Central America for several years. She was a good deal older, probably in her fifties, looking somewhat worn and earthy, right down to her brown leather sandals. The woman's long, gray hair fell in uneven waves and was full of snags, as if it hadn't been combed in years. She expressed a desire to write her memoirs, dedicated, of course, to the glory of God, which was why she was coming to God+Write. She introduced herself as Nell.

The lake never changes, thought Candi, as she stared out the window at the boaters and water skiers skimming across the water. A few more cabins had been built on the west side and there were now a couple of new stores and a restaurant across from the old Wallowa Lake Lodge when they reached the south side of the lake, and, of course, also the new tram station, with its clanking cables and whirring engines. There was more commercial activity than when she had been here as a girl. The small town of Joseph, with its broad streets, originally constructed to accommodate cattle drives through the heart of town, had now become artsy and touristy, with massive bronze sculptures by local artists graced some of the intersections, and new buildings housing art galleries. Clearly Joseph had been discovered by the outside world. But other than that, everything else seemed quite the same as she remembered from her summers here with the church group and Pastor Bob. Bowlegged cowboys, swaying on their high-heeled boots, could still be seen navigating the sidewalks, along with the out-of-towners and artists.

Candi breathed in the familiar heavy scent of pine and fir as she finally stretched her cramped body out of her seat and stepped from the bus. Once more she felt the crunch of pine needles beneath her feet. When all the passengers had left the bus they claimed their luggage and gear and were herded into the Great Hall of the campground administration building for an orientation meeting where Redd Benson welcomed them all, first with a prayer, which went on far too long, and then followed by the handing out of more packets of information. God+Write participants other than those who had come on the chartered bus were also on hand, as many of them had arrived by private car and were either going to live at the campground with the others, or had taken lodging elsewhere in the area motels or at the old lodge. There were at least three hundred people crammed into the Great Hall, all writers or would-be writers, ready and anxious to delve into the secrets of successful and hopefully lucrative careers in Christian literature. They longed to jump onto the Christian bandwagon. They knew that ten percent for Jesus meant ninety percent for them. That sounded like a good deal to them. There would be workshops in Christian fiction, Christian poetry, Christian essays, and memoir, as well as workshops on marketing one's work and finding a publisher and on e-publishing and self-publishing. Each day would begin with a worship service in the Great Hall, followed by breakfast in the adjoining dining hall. Each evening there would be a program of readings and lectures by the various faculty members, as well as by invited guest authors, after which there would be a closing vesper service conducted either by

Redd or, as Candi was surprised to learn, none other than Pastor Bob Fairly, still rotund and still just as horny looking as ever. She had not noticed him standing at the back of the room until Redd had introduced him as the new Chaplain in Residence to the conference and he had stepped forward to acknowledge the applause of the audience.

Despite the unexpected presence of Pastor Bob, Candi was amazed and thrilled by the unfolding scene. The faculty members for the conference, including Professor Kees, were standing around the perimeter of the Hall, rocking from one foot to the other, waiting also to be introduced. Candi eyed them all, wondering which one was the famous Viktor Karshenko. When after all the other faculty members had been introduced and had given a brief hand wave or nod to the conferees, Viktor was brought to the podium with much fanfare, a smiling elderly man who waved and bobbed his head in response to the reception that greeted him. The crowd clapped loudly for him and he took Redd's hand and, in words no one could understand, tried to express his great pleasure at being there. Candi noticed that he limped slightly when he came forward to acknowledge the crowd. She could see that he was wearing nice new hiking boots, however. And, despite his age, his limp and the fact that she couldn't understand what he had said, she was excited just to be in his presence.

Finally the gathering came to an end and each participant who was staying at the campground accommodations was assigned to a yurt to share with several others. Candi toted her luggage and gear to her assigned yurt, a round, canvas-covered structure with wooden walls, set deep in the forest behind the main building. Each yurt contained four bunkbeds and housed up to eight people. Candi was pleased to see that Nell, her companion on the bus trip, was one of the eight in her yurt. Each woman selected a bunkbed and set about unpacking. Candi recalled, somewhat wistfully, that she and Pastor Bob had once satisfied his need to express his love of God in a most carnal way behind this very structure. That experiece seemed almost prophetic now that Pastor Bob was once again part of the scene. Almost a second coming, she thought. He had not been on the bus, and she didn't know if he had seen her or even recognized her in the crowd.

There was about an hour before dinner, so Candi decided to explore some of the old haunts alone. She walked the quarter mile to the lake shore, through the state campground, following the raging course of the Wallowa River as it hurtled down the mountainside toward the open waters of the lake, crashing down from out the upper peaks, its water almost as cold as the snowfields from which it had been formed. Candi sat by herself on the lake shore watching the boaters and several men and boys fishing off the dock. She felt a sense of ease and relaxation settling over her, one she had not felt for a long, long time. Two weeks of this, she thought. No school. No lap dancing. No Nockers' Up-Town Bar and Grille. No Old Mel, or his kind. Just the peace and quiet of the wilderness that surrounded her. It seemed a miracle that she was here and it was all happening. A miracle, indeed. A gift from God.

CHAPTER 18

R USSELL KEES HAD BEEN SITTING HUNCHED DOWN IN THE BACK OF THE bus when he saw Candi come on board and take one of the few seats still empty near the front, just behind the driver. He didn't know if she had seen him or not. With Lucy off to Mt. Vernon that morning for the balance of the summer, he was already beginning to relax. The trip took most of the day, and there were very few stops along the way. Box lunches had been handed out before they left Portland, and at each stop the bus gained new passengers. He munched slowly on a tuna sandwich as they passed through Pendleton and the Umatilla Indian Reservation and began their ascent up over Cabbage Hill, winding up and up, past Emigrant Springs, and past Meacham. Ruts from the old Oregon Trail were visible and pointed out to them by the bus driver, who from time to time would get on the public address sound system to give them a history lesson about the areas they were passing through. Evidence of pioneer settlements was everywhere.

Finally by late afternoon the bus rounded the lake and rumbled into the campground. Russell was the last to leave the bus. He gathered up his luggage and laptop case and trailed the others into the Great Hall. Redd Benson was already holding forth on the dais, his arms spread out wide, his smiling, glowing face turned to the heavens, pleading for God to bless this conference and its conferees and faculty. The hall was jammed and Russell found a place along the far wall, next to several other faculty members. Soon, he, along with the others, was introduced and there was a smattering of applause as his few accomplishments in poetry were exaggerated for the benefit of the audience. He waved his hand in recognition and smiled. For a brief moment, he felt like the star. He could see Candi looking up at him from the sea of faces, her eyes shining with anticipation. She had an almost angelic look about her. It was far different than the cynical and distant look she had offered the crowd at Nockers' Up-Town Bar and Grille when he had seen her performing there earlier.

Finally, however, Viktor Karshenko, the true conference star, was introduced to uproarious applause and the old guy hobbled up to the front of the room and acknowledged the welcome. Russell didn't know much about Karshenko, although he had recently found and read a translation of a book of his poems, and had been impressed by them. He was looking forward to getting to know him personally. After all, he had never met a Nobel Prize winner before.

When the welcome session was over Russell went immediately to his assigned cabin, which, he was pleased to see, was right on the edge of the lake with a lovely view of both the entire lake and Mt. Howard rising in the background. To his further delight, he discovered that he had been billeted with Viktor Karshenko himself. The cabin actually belonged to a private owner who had rented it out to the conference as housing for faculty members and guests. It was comfortable but rustic. It was obvious that most of the cabins had been here for many years, and that there had been no such thing as land-use planning when they were constructed. Lots were of uneven sizes and cabins had been built in every which way, some large, some small, A-frames here, chalets there.

There was a knock on the door and Viktor came stumbling in, dragging his luggage behind him, his new backpack slipping from one side of his shoulders to the other, throwing him off balance. He dropped his bags to the floor. Russell rushed over to help him.

"I'm Russell Kees," he said, extending his hand after he had helped lift Viktor's suitcase onto the bed in the other bedroom. "I teach a workshop in poetry."

"Ah, Rushel," said Viktor, "I sho glat to now you." He took Russell's hand and shook it with more vigor than Russell would have expected for a man of his obviously advanced years. "Any Wodka around here? Viktor said. "I dying of turst."

CHAPTER 19

JESSE RED HAWK, AKA ZAFARELLI, WAS LONELY. THE SMALL, DANK ROOM he occupied at the Double Six was beginning to close in on him more and more. He thought of Candi and decided he should stop in at Nockers' Up-Town Bar and Grille and see what she was up to. He hated the work she was doing, the men ogling her and groping at her, but at the same time, he was fascinated by the lights and the atmosphere, the music at high volume, and the thought that he had at one time possessed what so many men now wanted. Candi.

It was a little past 10 p.m. when he slipped into the bar and found an empty table near the back. A tired looking, somewhat overweight blonde woman, close to middle age if she was a day, was working the pole as best she could, her vacant stare caught in the flashing strobe lights, flat and blank as a china plate. No one seemed to be paying much attention to her except for a group of college kids huddled in front of the stage area, watching her every move. Jesse motioned to the cocktail waitress, Beatrice, and ordered a beer, and watched while the dancer awkwardly twirled around the pole, back and forth, up and down with a sliding motion, trying her best to simulate sex and to make it seductive and exciting. Her efforts were so absurd that it almost made Jesse laugh out loud, horny as he was. Only the college boys were really captivated by her charms. When she finally reached a climax of sorts and worked her way down into the audience of men there was only a smattering of applause. Nor were there any takers for a table dance. Only the college students were interested, and they had no money. She soon disappeared into the backroom, while Jesse sipped his beer and waited in anticipation for Candi to appear. But there was no Candi.

It was an especially slow night and Big Cal had spotted Jesse when he first arrived. Cal had been keeping an eye on him. He didn't need any trouble from the ex-boyfriend of his favorite dancer. Candi had warned him about Jesse and the disturbing phone calls and contacts. At one point she had even contemplated trying to get a restraining order out on him. But she didn't want to spend the money on a lawyer. She could have found one sitting at the bar at any given moment, but she realized that they were all drunks and who needed that. Cal also knew that Candi wasn't here that night, in any event, and would not be here for at least the next two weeks. He didn't know if Jesse knew that or not. He assumed not. For Cal it was going to be a long two weeks with Candi gone. He felt a sudden longing to be back in the trailer watching the latest episode of the Larry Singer Show. It always calmed him down and made life look a little better to him.

"Hey, Jesse, what's up with you?" Big Cal leaned over the small, round table where Jesse was sitting, casting a huge shadow and blocking Jesse's view of the stage and bar. Jesse was quietly nursing his second beer.

Jesse looked up into Cal's broad, sweating face. He must be the ugliest son of a bitch on the face of the earth, he thought. "Not much, Cal. How's it hangin'?" Jesse sipped his beer some more while Cal settled into the chair across from him. He wasn't usually so friendly. In fact, he had never been this friendly before. Jesse felt a certain sense of suspicion coming over him. He squinted at Cal through the smoke and the glare of the bar and lit a cigarette. He was careful not to blow the smoke in Cal's face. Having Cal sitting there was like having a wall suddenly appear out of nowhere, completely blocking his line of vision.

"Where's Candi tonight?" he asked. "She not workin'?"

"Nah" Cal paused and stared into Jesse's eyes. "She's on vacation." He gave a little smirk, pleased that he knew something about Candi's life that Jesse obviously did not.

"Vacation? What vacation. What the shit does that mean? Since when do dance girls here get vacations?" Jesse was bewildered by the thought. He had never had a vacation in his life. He been laid off, fired, shit-canned, tossed into jail and generally fucked over. But he had never had a vacation. He struggled with the concept.

"Where'd she go? When's she comin' back?" He put his cigarette down in the ashtray and picked up his beer. Diana, another listless dancer had just appeared on stage. He could hear the music start up again, although he could barely see past Cal. He craned his neck to see around him but the girl was clearly not Candi.

"Yeah, she's up in the mountains somewhere. Something they call a "retreat," whatever the hell that is. A retreat for writers, she said. Gordie was really pissed off that she wanted the time off." Cal looked around and gestured at the near empty room. "You can see she was the real draw here."

"What the fuck's she doin' in the mountains? She's no mountain girl. Small town, that's for sure, but no mountain girl." Jesse emitted a weak laugh at the thought of the soft little college girl wandering around in some forest, getting it on with nature. He was the one who knew how to get it on with nature. It was in his Nez Perce blood.

Cal took a pack of cigarettes from the pocket of the bowling shirt he always wore when he was on duty, the one with his name embroidered over the pocket and "Turley's Hardware" on the back. He shook one out, put it to his lips, lifted Jesse's cigarette from the ashtray and lit his own. He sucked smoke deeply into his massive lungs and exhaled into Jesse's face. Jesse knew better than to protest. The glow from the tip highlighted Cal's broad, ugly face against the dark shadows of the barroom.

"It was somethin' to do with that school she goes to. Some writers' conference where they get together in the woods and write stuff. She got some sort of scholarship, she called it." He paused and took another drag on the cigarette, again blowing the smoke directly into Jesse's face. "She must be pretty smart."

If anyone but Cal had twice blown cigarette smoke in his face, Jesse would have risen to the challenge. His muscles tensed up. But he was not about to take on Cal.

"She's not as smart as she thinks she is," said Jesse. "She won't make any money up there." He repositioned himself as the dumpy middle-aged blonde came back onto the runway and the music blared up again. There were three off-duty cops who had come in and were now sitting at the front of the bar, next to the college boys. They turned from their watered-down drinks to cheer the poor lady on. No act, however poor, was too poor that the cops wouldn't enjoy it.

"Well, she took off on some chartered school bus with a whole bunch of other folks yesterday morning," Cal said.

"Did she say just where this conference was happenin'?" asked Jesse. The dancer had slipped while trying to get her leg up the pole, and one of the cops had leaped onto the stage to help her up. His pals were going nuts with laughter. Gordie Nockers stuck his head out the door of his office to see what was going on and turned away, groaning and holding his head. Another Workman's Comp claim on the way, he thought. Just what I need. He could see one of the lounge lizard lawyers sitting at the bar glowing with anticipation.

Cal didn't move from his chair. If it had been Candi in trouble up there he would have been up there in a flash. "She said it was at some lake up in the mountains of eastern Oregon. Some place she used to go to in the summers when she was a kid. I don't recall the exact name. Way to hell and gone. Almost to Idaho, she said."

"Wallowa Lake?" asked Jesse.

"Yeah, that could be it. There used to be some sort of Bible-thumper camp up there that she went to every summer when she lived back there." Cal drifted a perfect smoke ring up into the darkness; it was one of the few perfect things he could actually do.

"That's where it must be," said Jesse, as he drained the last of his beer. He had never been to Wallowa Lake; in fact, he had never been east of the Correctional Facility in Troutdale, on the outskirts of Portland. But he had read about it in his book on Indian life and thoughts of his newly beloved Nez Perce country suddenly loomed in his besotted mind. He looked closely at Cal, whose lump of a face was watching him with mild curiosity. He had always been more than a little afraid of Big Cal. Who wouldn't be? he thought. Just look at the big bastard sitting there like a ten story building. Only not as smart. While Jesse didn't know him well, he knew that he was also taken with Candi and that it was his job to protect all the girls in the club, like he was the secret service, or something. That was the right kind of muscle and fat to have on your side: stupid, but mean when it counted.

"You got wheels, Cal?" Jesse asked, as endearingly as possible, as he tried vainly to avoid the blanket of smoke coming from Cal's side of the table, as Cal lit yet another cigarette.

"Yeah, well, I got the old Honda out in the parking lot." He squinted at Jesse as his mind rumbled along in low gear. "Why?" He didn't trust Jesse any farther than he could throw him. Which would have been quite a ways, actually.

"My truck is temporarily in the hands of the law, since I'm still on probation for that last dee-wee. So, no truck, no license." He paused as the blonde dancer once again finished her set to very little applause from any of the few stragglers playing with their drinks and a few of them throwing darts at the dart board on the far wall, by the pool table. The one exception being the trio of cops making lewd remarks, grabbing at their crotches and slapping one another on the back. Even the college boys outranked them in maturity. "What say you and I make a run up to Wallowa Lake and check out what's happenin'? I'm not workin' at the moment," He grinned, "I'm on 'vacation', as they say."

Big Cal hesitated, taking in Jesse's proposal. "I don't know if I can get away. Gordie might fire me." He sucked deeply on his cigarette. "I was late the other day and he really chewed my ass out."

"Bullshit, Cal. They'd never fire you. You're the best bouncer they've ever had here. Trust me, Candi told me that. Besides, what if she needs some help up there? Some back up?" He was sure his use of a police reference, like "back up" would appeal to Cal. And it did.

Cal gave it some thought, which was never easy for Cal. He looked around at the empty tables. Even the cops were getting ready to leave. The place was dead. Another dancer, Julie, another student from East Hills Liberty, had come onstage. She had a little more energy than the aging blonde that preceded her. She actually began to leap disjointedly up and down the metal pole, twirling around.

Shit, she moves like a monkey fuckin' a football, Jesse thought, as he watched her movements with disdain, waiting for Cal's response.

"I guess it wouldn't hurt to ask Gordie if I could get a week or two off. There ain't much goin' on around here with Candi gone." He shook yet another cigarette out of his pack and lit it, again blowing a cloud of smoke directly into the face of Jesse Red Hawk, Indian warrior. Smoke signals, for sure, thought Jesse, coughing. "I'll ask and let you know."

"Okay, do that. You let me know. I'd hate to see her up there alone in the wilderness. She might really need us around."

Cal nodded and stood up to his full height and width, which gave Jesse the impression of a mountain suddenly moving on its very own, and gave him a thumbs up. In his dimming mind Cal was already Larry Singer coming to the rescue. He could almost feel the heat of the studio lights and the buzz of the unruly crowd, ready to cheer him on, as he waited just off stage to come on and relate his daring rescue of the lovely stripper, his dream girl, lost in the wilderness. After all, Candi might really be needing help. Who else would she call on but Big Cal, aka Larry Singer?

CHAPTER 20

RUSSELL WAS UP EARLY THAT MORNING. NOT BECAUSE HE WAS SO enamored with the setting and the scenery, but because his new roommate, Viktor, snored like a blast furnace. All night long he had rumbled and rattled, tossing and heaving in his bed. Every now and then he would yell out something in Russian, or at least Russell assumed it was Russian. Viktor sounded desperate, as if he were about to be beaten with whips. As a result, Russell slept very little, and having gotten to bed quite late to begin with he was very out of sorts by 6 a.m. when he staggered from the cabin to sit on a bench by the lake, a much needed cup of coffee in his hand. He was shivering with cold, but at least it was quieter.

He had to admit, the setting was idyllic. Deer had come down from the hills to the lake to drink and to feed. They were remarkably tame and a good-sized doe and her fawn came right up to him, begging for something to eat. He had nothing for them and was in no mood to be a lover of the wonders of nature and wild animals and he shooed them off with a wave of his hand. They skittered away. Even from here he could still hear Viktor rumbling away in the cabin, snorting loud enough to shake the curtains in the front window, with a few rumbling farts thrown in. The cabin sat facing the lake to the east, the lengthy moraine at its back, and the highway that circled the lake from the north, running along the east edge to the lodge and the other facilities.

Russell watched as early morning fishermen pushed off from the boat dock at the very south end of the lake. The water looked cold and black, with slight waves of silver shimmering across the surface. On the far side of the lake were other cabins but there was no sign of life from any of them. Behind them the rugged Wallowa Mountains rose majestically, capped with snow. A little more caffeine and he would finally begin to feel a little more human, he thought, as he pondered the scene. Viktor continued to make his presence known from afar.

Suddenly Russell saw two figures appear in the distance on the boat dock. One of them looked as though it might be Candi. The other was a woman he didn't know but thought he had seen on the bus yesterday, and again last night at the orientation. An older woman, an earth-mother sort. Not Candi's type, he thought. They sat down at the end of the dock and dangled their feet out over the water. Russell watched as they seemed deep in conversation, as if they had been friends for years.

Heavy footsteps behind him interrupted his thoughts, and his observation of Candi and her companion. Viktor sat down beside him with a thump. He had found the coffee and had a heavy steaming mug in his hand.

"Goot morning, Rushel," he said. "Did you shleep vell?"

Russell looked at him and shook his head. What could he say? "No, I guess I was too excited to be here," he answered, his eyes still fixed on Candi and her friend off in the distance. His eyes were red and rheumy. "I didn't sleep well at all."

"So sorry to hear that. I din shleep well myself. I don't know why they don have no wodka around here. What kind of conference is dish?"

Russell wasn't entirely sure what Viktor had said but recognized again the word "wodka." This was the first Christian conference he had been to where the guest writers were asking for booze. At that moment he could have used something stronger than coffee himself.

"I think I saw a liquor store next to the convenience store when we arrived on the bus yesterday. You could probably get something there." Viktor nodded his approval. "How do you like Wallowa Lake?"

"Ah, ishs lovely. Reminds me of a part of Siberia where I wash for several yearsh. Wild and beautiful." Viktor let out a series of coughs and sputters, clearing this throat and spitting a huge wad of gunk onto the bank. At the noise, three deer that had come down to inspect them raced back into the foliage. "Wonderful mountains." He took a cigar out of his vest pocket, unwrapped it, snipped off the end and lit it up. He puffed heartily to get it going, the smoke drifting over to Russell, who was doing his best to avoid it. With the cigar in his mouth Viktor began to relax.

Russell watched as Candi and her companion got up and left the boat dock and soon disappeared into the forest, heading back toward the campground. He looked down at his watch. It was time for morning services already. He had hoped the faculty would be exempt, but, with the exception of Viktor, they were not. These Christians show no mercy, he thought. Everyone else was expected to attend any and all services and vespers. But even the stalwart organizers of God+Write weren't going to drag an old Jew to Christian services. Lucky guy, thought Russell. I might have to convert to Judaism. Then I could at least sleep in. He rose from the bench and walked back toward the cabin, leaving Viktor immersed in cigar smoke, coughing and hacking, staring blissfully across the lake as the sun rose at his back.

CHAPTER 21

RUSSELL LOOKED OUT OVER THE GATHERING OF ANXIOUS, EXCITED faces that surrounded him in the Great Hall, where his first poetry workshop was to be conducted. It was the first morning of activities. He had placed chairs in a large circle, with his slightly elevated. He had passed out worksheets for the coming days, so that students who wished to could have specific exercises or writing projects to work on. Others, with work in progress, were free to offer their poems to the workshop for critique. Every day each participant would be taken in turn, around the circle, reading a poem and dispensing hard copies for the other participants. Each reading of a poem would be followed by comments, and critique, pro and con, from the students and, finally, from Russell. The participants had all been sent an exercise to prepare for the opening session. They were to write a poem about how God had blessed their lives. Candi and Nell sat with the others, clutching their shiny, new poems, waiting for Russell to begin.

"Good morning, poets," Russell intoned, as he eyed Candi sitting off to his right, noting that she was wearing the shortest pair of short-shorts he had ever seen. Hardly suitable dress for such a God-fearing girl, he mused. But nice, nevertheless.

"We will be going around the circle giving each of you the opportunity to read your poem for us. We will then allow time for anyone who so wishes to respond to it." Russell paused and looked around at the workshop participants waiting expectantly. "Then, I will have my say." He smiled enigmatically.

They all let out a groan in unison at that point. Ressell grinned his best East Hills Liberty grin, and went on. "Anyone who wishes to do so may have private sessions with me, one on one, and can just let me know after this morning's workshop and we can arrange for a get together. I will try to maintain regular office hours, although I don't really have an office up here. But I guess we can just commune with nature." He looked directly at Candi. He thought he saw her nod slightly. Encouraged, he went on.

"It is not our objective to denigrate or embarrass anyone." This was his standard pitch to workshops, especially workshops in poetry. "Please keep your critiques impersonal and to the point." He paused again. "Nor are we here to rewrite one another's poems. We are merely here to give each poet feedback as to how a particular poems works, or doesn't work, in our judgment. Each of us has his or her own voice. We do not want to destroy that sense of individuality."

He looked around the group again, taking in the expectant faces, some young, like Candi's, some not so young, like Nell's. He had read the registration forms and applications from each of the participants, as well as several of the poems each had submitted beforehand, and had some idea of their diverse backgrounds and accomplishments. While these backgrounds varied, their accomplishments, at least in poetry, were extremely limited. But that didn't bother Russell. He expected that. In fact, he hoped for it, given his own limited success as a published poet. After all, "Ode to the Salvation of a Woodcock" had not made it into the *New Yorker*. Or even into *Riches for God*, the official organ of the Pacific Northwest Evangelical Foundation, although the poetry editor, Pastor Rick Epsom, in his rejection slip, had said it was, in his words, "a mighty fine poem". He went on to say that he had to turn it down due to limited space. This was an excuse Russell had heard before. He had been encouraged by it nonetheless and was then pleased to have it finally accepted by *Heavenly Discourse,* making him, at last, a published poet, at least in the eyes of his students and the college administration.

"Let's go around the group and introduce ourselves," Russell continued. There is nothing more personal than the writing of poetry and we need to feel a sense of trust with one another. We are going to be in close contact for the next two weeks, both here and in the other conference activities, and we need to get to know something about each other. I know a few of you, but not most of you. So let's start here, on my right." Russell nodded to the young man seated next to him.

For the next two hours the group read their poems, and discussed each in detail, while Russell offered his expert advice at the end of each discussion of each poem. It was clear that God would certainly have been pleased with the results, as every poet had nothing but good things to say about Him. No one worried much about bad things happening, such as natural disasters, airliners dropping from the sky, infant mortality rates, or the like. God was uniformly portrayed as wonderful and filling their lives to overflowing with His blessings.

"This has been a wonderful start for our time together," said Russell, as he passed out another exercise for tomorrow's session. "For tomorrow we want you to write a poem about why you are a Christian. And in particular, why you are the Christian you are. No more than twenty lines, however." They grinned as one, nodding their heads. This one will be easy, they thought, too easy.

With that the workshop was dismissed for the day. The students scattered immediately, as there was another workshop on writing Christian fiction upstairs starting very shortly and they wanted to grab a bottle of water before it began. No one wanted to miss out on that workshop as they all knew that was where the real money was in Christian writing, the pot of gold at the end of God's rainbow, so to speak. Not in poetry, certainly. Fiction! That was the real heart and soul of Christian writing. Plot-lines about people finding both God and love (of a more earthly - but still moral nature) danced in their collective heads. Yes, at the end of that rainbow were riches of a more material kind as well as the usual rewards of heaven and salvation. After all, they reasoned, if you don't make a bundle on this earth while you can, how can you tithe in grand style? Ten percent for God always added up to a healthy remainder for the giver. And even that ten percent was tax deductable. It couldn't get any better than that. Was this a great, Christian nation, or what? So, off they went in search of water and manna from heaven.

Except for Candi. She remained behind. She cautiously approached Russell, as he had been hoping she would

"Professor Kees," she said. She touched him on the shoulder, as his back was turned to her.

Russell turned around and smiled broadly at his star pupil. "Please, just call me Russell up here. No more of that Professor Kees business."

She nodded. "Russell," she said, somewhat awkwardly, "I'd very much like to take you up on those one on one sessions you mentioned." She paused, a bit embarrassed. "I'm so uncertain about my poems."

"Well," he responded, "You certainly don't need to feel that way. Your poem this morning was delightful. Who would have thought that getting new patent leather shoes for your first Easter when you were a child would have been such ripe material for a poem."

They walked toward the doorway together. "I'd be happy to work with you. How about later this afternoon? Classes and workshops will be over by four o'clock and we could meet down by the lake for some quiet contemplation." He touched her elbow and smiled again. Lucy was getting farther and farther away. Mt. Vernon seemed more and more distant.

"Wonderful!" She almost squealed with anticipation. "I'll be right here at four o' clock sharp."

"I'll see you then," Russell said. He tried his best to maintain a professional expression on his face, but it wasn't easy. Candi turned to leave and he watched intently as her taut buttocks encased in the short-shorts, waved good bye to him. Although he had seen her at the club wearing even less than those short-shorts, he was nonetheless intrigued. Her poem that morning had, frankly, not been very good. In fact, it had been awful. But, then, it was not much worse than any of the others. And he was certain, with the proper coaching and personal attention, she would quickly improve. In Russells's mind, Mt. Vernon had just dropped off the face of the earth.

CHAPTER 22

THE ANCIENT HONDA CIVIC CHUGGED SLOWLY UP CABBAGE HILL, taking the curves with abandon. Exhaust smoke poured out from the rear end in a steady stream. Big Cal sat behind the wheel, one arm slung out the window, the radio blaring country-western music from a station in Pendleton. Jesse sat next to him, smoking weed and drinking one beer after the other from a case of Bud that lay at his feet. He'd snuffed up some good crank before they left, and his eyes were spinning around like little red orbs.

"How much farther we got to go?" he asked, as he glared over at Cal. He had a road map spread out on his lap that they had picked up at a Texaco station in The Dalles. He had tried to plot their trip but wasn't having much success. He had never been this far east before.

"That waitress cunt in Pendleton said when we get to La Grande we head northeast to Elgin and Enterprise. She said if we get on the right road we can't miss it 'cause that's the only place it really goes to, Wallowa Lake. Nothin' much beyond that."

Cal causally flipped another burning cigarette out onto the side of the road into the tall, dry grass. "So, watch for La Grande." He had never been this far east before either. He nodded his head in time to an old Johnny Cash number. Something about Fulsom Prison.

The landscape had changed dramatically once they had left the Gorge area, becoming more stark and spread out. And it was getting hotter. But Jesse knew in his fucked up heart of hearts that he was, somehow, returning to his ancestral home, Nez Perce country. He kept thinking that he would see something familiar at any moment. Jimmy Eagle Feather would be proud of me, he thought. He had learned his lessons well. He was going home at last. Thanks, in an odd way, to Candi.

Unfortunately, the old Honda wasn't so sure or so pleased to be pushing its way east. Coughing worse than Jesse was from bad Indian grass, the car slowed and chugged finally to a halt and Big Cal had to pull it off to the side of the road. They both got out, and Cal raised the hood and they stared despairingly at the dying engine. It coughed once more in protest just to make sure they understood how sick it was and finally gave up the ghost. Cal and Jesse stood in a cloud of exhaust and looked back down the mountainside toward the Umatilla Indian Reservation. Huge semis rumbled past, slowly working their way up the steep incline, adding to the foul air. Cal and Jesse tried vainly to get the attention of a sympathetic driver. One look at Cal and no one stopped. They were on their own.

Finally Jesse got reception on his cell phone and called for a tow truck to come out from Meacham. It was going to be a long wait. Hours, at best, he was told. They both got back into the Honda, its sagging springs groaning with Big Cal's weight, and sat passing the time. Hank Williams was now singing an old song about, of course, lost love, while they both drank the last of Jesse's case of beer and smoked the last of their cigarettes and some of the good B.C. bud that Jesse had brought. This trip was turning to shit, Jesse thought, as he cradled the last of a roach between his yellowed fingers and stared over at Cal. So much for vacationing.

So much for trying to protect Candi, thought Big Cal, wishing he was back at Nockers'.

The tow truck finally arrived and they were towed to a run-down repair shop in Meacham, some miles up the road, where a grizzled old guy, taking his time, patched the car back together again and at least got them up and running. With most of their reserve of cash, which hadn't been great to begin with, now depleted with the tow and the half-assed repair job, they hit the road again. They snaked over the mountains and finally down into the Grande Ronde Valley, down toward La Grande, following the course of the Grande Ronde River. They had enough money left to replenish their supply of cigarettes and beer, and Jesse was now working on another case of Bud at his feet. Cal had gotten a credit card from Sylvie at the club, one she had lifted from a drunk Shriner a couple of nights before. They could try to use that for a motel. For the time being, all seemed right with the world again.

"Turn off there," yelled Jesse suddenly, over the wail of the radio and Big Cal singing along with Loretta Lynn, as they entered La Grande. Jesse was getting damned tired of Big Cal's choice of music. In fact, he was getting damned tired of Big Cal. He pointed to the exit ramp from the I-84, and the sign indicating the route to Elgin and Enterprise. It was getting late in the day and the sun was rapidly setting at their backs when they took the highway out of La Grande, through Island City and out into the openness of the valley. They drove through seemingly endless acres of farmland and ranchland. They had at least another seventy miles to go. Assuming the old Civic could make it. The landscape had flattened out and they were going past vast wheat crops and open pastures. The Wallowa Mountains loomed before them in the distance, snow-capped and ominous.

Cal and Jesse stopped in Elgin for supper at a small diner on the main drag and then continued on northeast through Minam and Wallowa and Enterprise. Town after town seemed vacant and silent. By the time they rolled into Joseph it was dark and the town had already drifted off to sleep. It was a Monday evening and the streets were both wide and empty. Not a soul to be seen. A few cars were parked at the curbs, but no traffic and no apparent action.

"This don't look like much of a town to me," muttered Big Cal, looking up and down the nearly vacant main street. "Shit, look at that big son of a bitch." He pointed to a massive bronze statue sitting at an intersection, a statue of a pioneer and his covered wagon heading west, as they approached what appeared to be the center of the commercial part of town. The streetlights gave the bronze figures an eerie glow.

As they neared the southern end of the town Jesse pointed off to his right. "There's a motel. Let's pull 'er in for the night." The Indian Chief Motel sat back from the street, a U-shaped, single story older complex, its neon sign depicting a giant Indian warrior on a horse holding his spear beckoning to them, and the "Vacancy" sign flashing off and on. "It don't look too pricy," Jesse said. That was, to put it mildly, an understatement.

Cal pulled the old Honda into the parking lot and parked in front of the office. Jesse went in to book them a room, the cheapest one he could get. Cal waited in the car. Jesse didn't want him scaring the desk clerk, especially with him using a hot card. It's like having Bigfoot with me, he thought, as Cal parked the Honda in front of their room, the one closest to the highway on the very end of the building. They unloaded what luggage they had - which wasn't much - and settled down in the room. It was musty and dark and didn't appear to have been occupied for some time. Thankfully, thought Jesse, there were two single beds and he wouldn't have to shack up with Cal. The idea that he might inadvertently roll over on him in his sleep had occurred to Jesse.

At least they were finally here. Jesse shivered a bit from the cold and turned on the wall heater to try to get some warmth into the place. Even though it was July, it was still cold at night. He rolled a joint and walked out of the room for a last breath of mountain air and starred up at the Eastern Oregon night sky, blazing with stars. A moon hung over the darkened peaks of the Wallowas with a deep, orange clarity. Ah, he thought in his marijuana-befuddled mind, Nez Perce country. He could feel it in his bones. He could sense it in his blood. Home at last. He was a long way from being a Zafarelli now. He took a deep drag of that good bud and held it in as long as he could. Then he exhaled and he could feel his Indian ancestry coming at him from all sides saying, "Yes, Red Hawk, you're home. You're finally home."

CHAPTER 23

I T'S ALL COMING TOGETHER BEAUTIFULLY, THOUGHT REDD BENSON, AS he gazed out over the group sitting in the dining hall, adjacent to the Great Hall. Grace had been offered by Pastor Bob Fairly, and the conferees were having dinner together in a spirit of Christian fellowship. The tuition checks and credit card vouchers had almost all cleared the banks, showing the effort this year to be more than a little profit-making, for a non-profit venture, and his board of directors would be more than pleased by his work to date. He might even be in line for a raise, something he could certainly use. Although there was very little on which to spend money in this god-forsaken place. There was a tavern or two in Joseph, but he did not like to be seen frequenting such places of sin. One never knew who else might also be lurking around and would see him. Perhaps a trip over to the Pendleton Round-up in the fall would be in order once the conference responsibilities were behind him for the summer and the last of the goody-goodies had gone home. He loved the casino over there. The $9.95 prime rib dinner was the best anywhere. Local beef. That and a good roll in the hay with one of the working girls, one of the so-called "cowgirls of the night", over from Portland for the occasion, would be just the ticket. Everything at the conference was going off without a hitch. Even that oddball Russian had showed up, all the way from the Ozarks. No one knew what the old bastard ever said, but he seemed happy to be here. God knows, he ate like there was no tomorrow.

I wish I were happy to be here, thought Redd, as he gulped

down a plate of stir-fried tofu (a meat substitute that disgusted him) along with Thai noodles and a bowl of sticky rice on the side. Whoever eats this shit, he wondered? He was in a contemplative mood, however, as he drank a huge mug of decaf coffee. He always drank decaf coffee. The doc had told him he had to as his blood pressure was already sky high. Can't be too careful with your health and the old ticker, he had been told. Redd was sitting off by himself in an alcove mostly reserved for staff and faculty, although the faculty was encouraged to mingle with the peasants as much as possible, just to give them some sort of sense of being important enough to consort with. Next to him, off to one side, was the book table where a pleasant lady from a local Christian bookstore in Enterprise had set up a display to sell copies of the books written by the faculty and by any students who might have been previously published, of which there were a few. Yet another little money making endeavor, as Redd and maybe God+Write got fifteen percent of all sales. The authors got to autograph their books for the buyers, which gave them a certain feeling of celebrity; the bookstore made a small profit for selling them, and the buyers got a personalized souvenir to put in their home libraries that they would probably never look at again, let alone actually read. A reminder of their time here. And Redd didn't have to lift a finger. It was working out great.

"Students. Students." Redd finished off the last of his coffee and rose to his feet. He tapped the side of his mug until he finally had the attention of the entire room. At last every eye was on him. He cleared his throat.

"Tonight we have the pleasure of a fine poetry reading by Russell Kees. Russell, as most of you know, is a widely published poet from East Hills Liberty College, near Portland, a wonderful, God-driven institution of holiness. We will gather in the Great Hall at 8 p.m. sharp for the reading, which will be followed by a panel discussion on *The Trinity and the Creative Process, how to triple your selling power as a Christian writer*. No one will want to miss that.

That will be followed by Vespers which will be a fine way to say adios to a lovely day of enjoying God's grace. And then we expect you to all be in your beds by 10 p.m., getting your rest for another active day." He paused, grinning wickedly. "Your own beds, that is."

There was a slight ripple of nervous laughter as the students looked at one another, feigning shock. Redd grinned at his own devil-may care wit. Proof, he thought, that Christians are not stodgy folk but can yuck it up with the best of them. In fact he had seen a couple of gals here and there that he wouldn't have minded bedding for the night. For instance, there was that really cute little bundle of pussy in the front row with the short-shorts. But then he quickly remembered Texas and all the unfortunate events and accusations that had repeatedly rolled out over the airwaves across the entire country time and time again, and he contained himself. He was not going to screw up again. As God is my witness, he thought.

"So, please return here by 8 p.m. ready for a wonderful evening of God-inspired poetry." With that Redd sat down and turned his attention to the last of his tofu. Shit, he thought, as he turned a limp piece over with his fork, and examined at it closely. Who the hell ever thought this tasteless crap was food?

CHAPTER 24

R USSELL WAS CLEARLY NERVOUS, BUT HE DID HIS BEST TO HIDE IT. HE had given poetry readings before, of course, but never to such a large group. Usually it was only a few students or stragglers from the sub-culture of the local poetry scene crammed together in a coffee shop or wine bar somewhere. And never had he read in front of such a distinguished smattering of literary headliners such as Viktor Karshenko. He had gone over his notebooks of poems, trying to develop some sort of cohesive reading order that would impress his audience, but so far nothing was floating to the surface. He knew for certain, of course, that he would end with his blockbuster poem, his *Ode to the Salvation of a Woodcock*. That always brought the house down. But now he needed something just as stirring for an opener. He only wished he had been able to publish a book of poems, or at least a small chapbook. But so far he had not scored on that count. He had sent his manuscript of poems to numerous publishers as well as a few of those contests advertised in the writers' magazines, the ones offering publication to the winner, but so far had received nothing but rejections or, worse, silence. All the magazines had done was cash his checks for reading fees. It had been discouraging. This might very well be his break-through moment, his best opportunity to impress important people in the literary world. Such as Viktor Karshenko, who was now also his roommate for the next two weeks. Viktor was, after all, a Nobel Prize winner, someone revered in the larger world-wide literary landscape far beyond East Hills Liberty College in Oregon City, Oregon. He was beginning to think that there might really be a God after all. Well, he would just take his notebooks with him and see what seemed to be working with the audience. Play it by ear, as his own on-line instructor had told him so many times. Play it by ear.

The Great Hall was jammed when he arrived, not only with anxious students and less anxious faculty, but also with members of the general public, local folk glad to find some free entertainment for an evening, even if it was a poetry reading. After all, if all else failed, there was usually punch and cookies in the end, there for the asking. The folding chairs had been placed in long rows facing the lectern, which was slightly elevated. The Great Hall, like all the permanent buildings in the campground, was rustic and woodsy, a high chalet-style ceiling with hand-hewn wooden beams criss-crossed overhead, and plain cedar siding with deer horns adorned the walls. A long, crosscut saw, a relic of the old days of logging, the blade painted with a scene of the lake and the Wallowa Mountains in the background, hung over the huge, stone fireplace. An old, out-of-tune upright piano sat off to one side, used mostly for hymn playing during the worship services. It added a rather strange, bar-room tackiness to what should otherwise have been a worshipful atmosphere. The kitchen staff was still cleaning up in the dining room next to the Great Hall, and there was the occasional clatter of dishes being loaded into the dishwasher which could be heard above the rumble of the crowd waiting for the reading to begin.

"Please come to order," called out Redd Benson, as he stood at the lectern and tapped on the microphone with his pen to get the attention of the audience. The crowd quieted down almost immediately.

"It is my great pleasure to present our reader for this evening." Redd continued " The first reading of our conference. After a brief intermission the reading will then be followed by a panel discussion on the subject of how poetry serves the mission of God." Redd paused to look down at his notes. "Russell Kees teaches creative writing and poetry at East Hills Liberty College, one of the finest Christian colleges in the United States, an institution of higher learning with the highest of standards and the deepest commitment to the glory of God." His voice rose with the last utterance and he felt himself back in his old television preacher's mode, and he pounded the dais for emphasis. Just like the old days. "Mr. Kees holds a Master of Fine Arts degree in creative writing and has published poetry in such literary magazines as *Heavenly Discourse*. We are honored to have him with us. Please give a God-fearing welcome to a God-fearing poet, Russell Kees."

The crowd clapped loudly and Russell stepped forward. He laid his notebook on the lectern and gripped its sides as he looked out over the sea of expectant faces. He smiled shyly, a trick he had learned from watching the soap opera, "Days of Our Lives," and noticed Candi sitting in the front row, her face also upturned and entranced. He felt a sudden burst of energy. Maybe this was God's will in action, he thought.

"For my first selection," Russell began, "I would like to read a relatively new poem, in keeping with the holy adventure that lies before us. It is called *Dancing with God*. I wrote this poem on the bus coming up here. I feel so blessed to be here with you."

He lifted his notebook with both hands and held it out so that he could project his voice to the back of the Great Hall.

Dancing With God

Oh, God, how you dance on my soul
As the twilight shudders down
And Your Spirit comes over me.
Oh, God, how the music begins
Just as You have touched my heart.
Your Spirit knows my every need.
Oh, God, how you dance on my soul,
Your very Living Word living where I need it most.

Russell's voice echoed through the room, reverberating off the deer horns and the cedar siding. The sound system caught every word, every syllable, every nuance of meaning, and projected it out across the enraptured audience before him. He was beginning to feel a power he had never felt before, even when standing before a class of willing students. This was the power to move people, to literally hold them in the palm of his hand. With each poem the crowd clapped louder and louder. And Russell read on and on, each poem building to a new crescendo of meaning and depth. What could be more perfect for him," he thought, as he gazed in wonder about the Hall? Lucy in Mt. Vernon for the summer tending to the old folks, here he was facing a more than appreciative audience. And right there in the front row was Candi, her face glistening with excitement. And he was responsible for it. All of it. He felt like a god himself.

Russell capped his reading with his ever popular *Ode to the Salvation of a Woodcock,* and at the conclusion the audience rose as one to give him a standing ovation. He had never had such a literary triumph in his life. He felt he must have died and gone to heaven. And where better to do something like that than at the God+Write Christian Writing Conference.

Then, following the intermission, there was the panel discussion, *"The Trinity and the Creative Process,"* or, in other words, *"how to make a killing with Christian lit,"* but Russell was too elated by his own performance to stay. He slipped out the side door and walked slowly through the darkness to his cabin. There was only a few street lamps on the narrow road leading from the campground back down to the lake's edge and the cabin. He passed the motels and a restaurant, passed the tram's now empty gondolas gently swinging in the night air, waiting for tomorrow morning to resume again their slow and awkward ascent up and down Mt. Howard their machinery now silent. He felt as though he could walk on air. He felt he could ascend Mt. Howard himself, without a tram. Just climbing on air.

For the longest time Russell sat on the porch of the cabin alone and watched the black water of the lake rippling and moving quietly. There were no boats out on the water that he could see. Just those still moored to the dock, slowly knocking against one another in the dark. No one else was around. He could hear the rushing waters of the Wallowa River crashing down off the mountainside and pouring finally into the lake. It was the only sound, other than his own breathing and his heart pounding in the afterglow of his reading. He sat and looked up at the stars blanketing the night sky. As the darkness descended over him there was increasingly that high mountain chill in the air. But he didn't notice the cold. His performance was still keeping him warm.

CHAPTER 25

Nez Perce country. The Wallowa Mountains. Jesse, now Jesse Red Hawk, felt he had truly come home at last. He had read some of the history of the Nez Perce in their traditional lands in the Wallowas. He had read the saga of Old Chief Joseph, now buried at the north end of the lake, and also of Young Chief Joseph, his son. He knew young Chief Joseph's surrender speech to the U.S. government by heart. It was the only thing he had ever memorized in his entire life: "Hear me, my chiefs, I am tired. My heart is sick and sad. From where the sun now stands, I will fight no more forever." Jesse almost wept at the mere thought of these words.

He lay in the dark of the motel room, smoking and contemplating his family's Native American past. Of course, there was no Native American past. He had conjured it up, despite the fact that his parents disavowed the entire notion. What did they know, he thought? His father, Gino, was certain that Jesse had lost his mind. How could any good Italian kid turn his back on the Pope, Sophia Loren, or worse yet, pizza? Gino was sure Jesse's cultural betrayal was from smoking too much of that "funny stuff," as he called it. His mother too hoped he would someday come to his senses and once again be the olive-skinned Italian son to whom she had given life and raised as a good Catholic boy - even if there had been some very rough spots along the way.

Across the room Big Cal was snoring like a chain saw, his huge bulk heaving back and forth and up and down on the bed. It was a wonder it didn't collapse. What a dumb asshole, thought Jesse, as he lit another cigarette. He looked wistfully at the empty beer bottles lined up on the dresser. They had run out a couple of hours ago. He casually wafted a gigantic smoke ring into the air and watched as it drifted up against the ceiling and broke apart. He had even been forced to watch that fucking Larry Singer show on the TV for the first time in his life last night. It was awful. All about obese, defrocked priests with sexual fantasies about male African pygmies. Thank God I was able to get us a room with two beds, he thought. The idea of bunking down with Cal was more than he could stomach. Just seeing Big Cal disrobing was, in itself, enough to make you want to toss your cookies. But, Jesse conceded, Cal had the wheels and he didn't. The old Honda. Such as it was. And his size could come in handy at some point. But he was one giant asshole.

Jesse drummed what he thought was an ancient, Native American rhythm he had learned from Jimmy Eagle Feather while in the slam, his fingers thumping on the bedside table while he plotted what their next move should be. First of all, he needed to make sure Candi was here and okay. Maybe tomorrow they could scout out the conference grounds where she was supposedly staying. This alone sounded very Native American to Jesse. Scouting out the campground. The enemy. The mere thought energized him. In his mind's eye he could see himself moving through the trees like a shadow, pursuing his ancient ways, watching without being seen. He wondered what Young Chief Joseph would have done? "I will fight no more forever". Joseph's final words flashed through his mind.

Fuck that, he thought, as he stubbed out the remains of his cigarette and pulled the covers up over himself. Tomorrow the Great Spirit rides.

CHAPTER 26

CANDI AND NELL HAD JUST SETTLED IN FOR ANOTHER WORKSHOP, THIS one on writing freelance Christian articles in support of a total ban on abortions or of any form of birth control. They had been told that there was a great need for such articles all across the country, and religious magazines of all sorts were looking for new material, and while the pay was often nominal or nonexistent in most instances, the opportunities for publication and the building of a resume for the acceptance of future articles were terrific. The instructor, it happened, was no other than Pastor Bob Fairly.

Candi had been more than surprised to see Pastor Bob here at God+Write and again now, here, leading this workshop. Or any workshop, for that matter. She had not been aware that he was an author of any sort. She knew, of course, something of his other skills and attributes, but not that he was a writer. Little did she know that he was leading this workshop simply because the conference leadership, ie, Redd Benson, wanted to save money wherever possible, and, since Pastor Bob was already on staff as the conference Chaplain, a position whose duties that were not likely to overwhelm him, this responsibility was added to make the conference dollar go a bit further. After all, Viktor Karshenko didn't come cheap. Even if Pastor Bob did.

Pastor Bob came lumbering into the workshop toting a huge briefcase, stuffed to overflowing. Candi had seen little of him since his secretive undercover mission to expose smut at Nockers' Up-Town Bar and Grille, although she had caught a glimpse of him

at the orientation session and had seen him at the worship services. He had seemed oblivious to her at the bar where she had
lap-danced for him in the dark, with the strobe lights glaring in his
eyes (for what turned out to be a meager tip) and she wasn't certain he had even recognized her. If he had, he gave no indication of
it. She wasn't sure he recognized her now, although he might have,
since this was the location of his role in her initial seduction. Her
deflowering, so to speak. It was déjà vu all over again, she thought.
She wondered if he would recognize her now. He had not changed
to any great extent since that first night, years ago, in the darkened
pantry of this very building. He was still fat, only more so. Clearly,
his clerical difficulties had not diminished his desire for food. His
proclivity for polyester leisure suits and Day-Glo remained consis-
tent, however. Even here, in this rustic setting of Wallowa Lake and
the campground, he was dressed in a yellow and gray checkered
leisure suit, something not seen in the modern world in decades,
with a colorful Hawaiian shirt, showing beneath the open jacket,
the collar pulled up. Several heavy, fake gold chains hung around
the fat folds of his neck, and a huge knock-off Rolex watch glittered
from his chubby wrist; the zircons on the dial catching the shafts of
sunlight that filtered down through the high dusty windows. Yes, it
was the same old Pastor Bob, Candi thought, still as conservative
and retiring as ever.

Nell nudged her. "Get a load of him," she said, pointing to
Pastor Bob. "He must think he's a holy roller." She laughed at her
own joke.

Candi gave a watery grin and nodded. She hadn't told anybody
about her past history with the good Pastor Bob.

"Class, let's get started," began Pastor Bob. " Will you please
come to order? Please take your seats. May I suggest we begin our
work for the Lord with a prayer to Almighty God, asking that He
bless our efforts today,"

Pastor Bob looked around the circle of faces. He saw Candi and
immediately something deep inside stoked a fleeting memory. He

had seen that girl before. But where? He looked again. Pretty, for sure. Short-shorts. Very short-shorts. Hard to forget. Then it struck him full on. He gulped and looked again just to be sure. Yes, they had met at this very campground. This very building, on this very campground. They had more than met. Because of her his career had taken turns he had not wished for. Suddenly he began to sweat profusely into his favorite Hawaiian shirt. The one he had bought at Hilo Hattie's with a discount coupon in Kona just last year while he was serving as a volunteer at the summer session of the Many Nations' University, an unaccredited school that claimed to prepare missionaries to go out and spread the Word to the downtrodden of the world. The trip had given him an excuse to enjoy the beaches of the Big Island for two months and it gave him a tax write-off at the same time. Not bad planning, he had thought at the time. He wondered if this girl had recognized him. Of course she would. He was, after all, a noted figure in the world of religious leaders. His deodorant was beginning to fail as he took yet another peek at Candi, sitting there looking so innocent. This could be trouble, he thought. Trouble with a capital "S."

Suddenly Pastor Bob's opening prayer took on a greater urgency that he had anticipated. "Oh Dear God," he prayed, wringing his hands and looking up at the high, pointed ceiling of the hall, the dust motes floating like small clouds above him. "Dear God, bring Your Grace down upon these dear students as they wrestle with the issue of the sin of abortion, that they may bring to others the Good News of Your salvation and Your absolute hatred of those who advocate such abominations. We pray that you bring Your wrath upon all who engage in such vile practices. May they burn in hell for eternity." Pastor Bob was warming to the task, and his colorful Hawaiian shirt was now drenched in sweat. "And may You guide the pens of these godly writers as they seek to do Your Will. Bring the words to their minds, lips and hearts that will turn the souls of this nation to Your Path." With a huge sigh, he brought his oration to a close. "In the name of Jesus, our Lord and Master,

Amen, Amen." Pastor Bob could have gone on but he decided that he'd better stop before he got himself so worked up his shirt might be completely ruined and disintegrate. He had no plans to be back in Hawaii any time soon.

As the prayer concluded Candi lifted her eyes; for a moment she and Pastor Bob looked directly at one another. He's no Russell Kees, she thought, staring at his round, flabby, sweat-soaked face. But she couldn't help noticing the cool Hawaiian shirt he was wearing.

CHAPTER 27

Jesse and Big Cal had just finished a gigantic breakfast at the Round 'em Up Restaurant and Bar, plates overflowing with chicken fried steak, eggs over easy, hash browns, biscuits and gravy, and enough coffee to keep them awake for a millennium.

"Let's head over to the other side of the lake and check out the scene," said Jesse. Cal nodded, his huge mouth still crammed with biscuit, a little gravy dribbling down one side of his chin, working its way south through his goatee.

They got into the old Honda and Cal cranked it up, smoke pouring from the rear end. Soon they were heading south out of town and curving along the north side of the lake, then heading east.

"Look!" yelled Jesse, as they passed a sign off to the right, over-looking the northern edge of the lake, announcing the gravesite of Old Chief Joseph. He was pointing toward the parking area. "We gotta stop here. Pull it over, Dude."

Cal skidded to a stop and parked the car off the highway. There was no one around. They got out and walked the short path to the site of the memorial. There was the grave stone with its lettering and spread around the stone small mementos that visitors had left, totems of various kinds, souvenirs, mostly of Native American interest and origin. The grandeur of the lake appeared in the background. Jesse feft like falling to his knees. Never had he felt such a closeness to his past, however illusory. He was overwhelmed. Big Cal stood back and watched, not sure how he should be reacting.

The site meant nothing to him. It was just a hunk of stone and a bunch of junk scattered about, the grass mostly overgrown. But dumb as he was, he was still smart enough to keep his big mouth shut. He hadn't yet quite figured out how to take Jesse and his need to be an Indian. Except for the ponytail and the recent tattoos of Native American designs, he looked a lot alike any of the other Italian guys he had known. And he'd eaten a lot of pizza in his time. But then, suddenly, Jesse began to moan and beat his hands on his sides and dance around. Big Cal quickly looked over his shoulder to see if anyone else was around. Holy shit, he muttered to himself. Thankfully they were still alone. Well, let the crazy bastard do what he wants. No skin off my balls, he thought.

Back on the road, they passed to the east side of the lake and followed the shoreline for several more miles. It was a clear day and the lake was a deep, iridescent blue, sparkling in the sun. Even Big Cal was impressed. Boaters were out on the water and they could see people swimming and diving from floating platforms that were a hundred feet or so from the shore. Finally, they drove past the old Wallowa Lake Lodge that stood in elegant silence at the very southern end of the lake, a graceful old two story wooden structure that looked as though it had been there for many, many years. Pristine green lawns stretched out from the rear of the lodge down to the shoreline, and lounge chairs were scattered about for the relaxation of the guests. They could see people sitting quietly, drinking their morning coffee and reading newspapers, and gazing out at the beauty of the lake. It could have been a scene from the twenties. Across from the Lodge was a restaurant and a convenience store. Other amenities, including even a go-cart track, took up the space on the other side of the road. At the far end of the road was a state campground with RVs and pitched tents spread out in various campsites. At the intersection, a sign for the conference campground and center pointed them onto a road going farther south. They drove past more buildings, another restaurant, motels and the boarding site for the tram, which was already in operation for the day, rattling and shuddering as the cables groaned and the pulleys turned. The parking lot was full of cars and people were lined up to get on the gondolas as they came swinging down off the mountain, circled around the boarding platform and were held by workmen so that passengers could climb on and begin their ascent back up the steep slope, swaying above the clear-cut of trees.

"That'd scare the shit outta me," Cal said, as he watched the people pushing and shoving one another to get into the gondolas. "I hate heights."

"Ah, it's nothin' to be scared of," said Jesse. "Course, if I weighed in like you, I'd be fuckin' concerned that the whole fuckin' thing would come down." He laughed at the thought of Cal and the gondola crashing to the ground.

Big Cal just looked at him and turned away. Jesse was beginning to get to him.

Another few miles and they came to a one-lane, gravel road to the right. There was another sign for the campground and conference site. They turned off and soon crossed over a narrow, wooden bridge that spanned the Wallowa River. The entrance to the campground was on the other side, backed up again a wooded cliff. There were also an assortment of private cabins sitting at odd angles to one another. Cal stopped the car just outside the parking lot and they sat for a while, smoking and just looking into the campground. They could see, off among the trees, the main building, nearly hidden by the denseness of the forest. The parking lot was almost filled with cars, pick-up trucks and one aging yellow school bus. They could see people rushing in and out of the main building, many wearing bookpacks on their backs or slung over their shoulders.

"Let's leave the car here and walk around," said Jesse, as he snubbed out his cigarette in the ashtray and opened the door. He got out and looked around, wondering how Jimmy Eagle Feather might do this. How could he fade into the foliage and not be noticed by anyone? They hadn't taught him any of this sort of stuff in the books he'd read.

Cal then pulled the car off the roadway and parked it in a level, grassy space, turned off the motor and he too got out of the car and followed Jesse past the entrance to the campground. Jesse was crouched down and moving stealthily from tree to tree. Cal tried his best to imitate him. Cal felt ridiculous. As though he was back in high school.

"What the shit you doin'?" Cal asked.

"Shhh, you asshole," Jesse whispered, putting his forefinger to his lips. "We need to sneak up on 'em and see what they're doin'." Jesse didn't want to accidently run into Candi. Not now, at least. She'd be pissed as hell. Cal shook his massive head. It wasn't easy to be Larry Singer up here in the mountains. Not with this crazy fucker who thought he was an Indian. The hot lights of Hollywood seemed suddenly an awful long way's away.

CHAPTER 28

CANDI SAT BENEATH A LARGE FIR TREE AT THE LAKESHORE CLUTCHING her notebook of recent poems. It was late afternoon and her workshops were over for the day. She was waiting for her first private one on one consultation with Professor Kees, now to be called Russell. He had been very kind to offer to meet with her and go over some of her poems. She felt so unsure of herself in his poetry workshop as she was such a novice at the art. She had written poetry for years but had never had the nerve to share any of her poems with anyone else, much less a professor and published poet like Russell Kees. The other students, such as Nell, all seemed far more advanced, compared to her. And, of course, Professor Kees was widely published and well known as a poet.

"Candi," called Russell, as he approached her. "Are you ready for our private one on one?"

"Oh, yes," responded Candi, as Russell sat down beside her.

Russell did not fail to notice that Candi was not wearing her short-shorts now but rather more demure but still quite tight-fitting jeans, as well as a cotton blouse that fell open at the front, revealing just a hint of cleavage. He wasn't entirely disappointed.

"Well, let's see what you have." He took a sheet of paper from his jacket pocket. "The poem you brought to the workshop was really quite good." Russell held up his copy of her poem, on which he had written some suggestions and comments. It was entitled, *God Is My Way And My Light*. "I've gone over it several times and made some notes and observations." He paused. "Unlike some of

the others in the workshop, I think you have some real talent."
Suddenly he found himself swimming in the deep blue of her eyes.
He bent over her to share his copy of the poem. He could see that
she was wearing a pair of flip-flops on her delicate feet, and her
toenails were painted a brilliant red. As he swam deeper and deeper
into her innocent face he could vaguely remember having been
married at one time, but it no longer seemed very important. After
all, dear Lucy was off to Mt. Vernon. On the other hand, he could
recall the marketing slogan from Las Vegas,something about what
happens in Vegas staying in Vegas. That slogan was beginning to
have more immediate meaning for him now. Suddenly he was so
close to her that he could actually smell the residue of shampoo in
her long, dark hair.

Candi, too, could smell Russell's cologne, a heavy musk in
which, she thought, he must have drenched himself. Frankly, it
was a little overpowering. Combined with the scent of his Old
Spice deodorant and his Aqua Velva aftershave, and his hair gel, a
product whose scent she hadn't encountered before, the effect was
an asphyxiating combination of odors. She felt a powerful head-
ache coming on. She was reminded of some of the construction
workers who came to the bar in the late afternoon, and who tried
to mask their pungent, end-of-the-workday body odor with various
concoctions. It never quite worked, and she sometimes found herself gagging during those close encounters for a private lap dance.
But Professor Kees – now Russell to her - was a different sort of
man. Cultured. Sophisticated. She could put up with a bit of musk.
And here, in the great outdoors, it was, perhaps, less intense.

"Now, here I would consider making a line break," he was
saying as he leaned even closer, pointing to the third stanza of the
poem. "That will make a nice emphasis on the word "heaven" and
give you a good syllable count as well, maintaining the rhythm of
the line."

She nodded, overcome by his knowledge of such matters as line
breaks and syllable counts. She hesitently took several more poems

from her notebook for him to read through. But then, suddenly, his hand was on her thigh. It was just there, gently rubbing the taut denim of her jeans. It seemed almost as if he were unaware he was doing it.

"Professor Kees, er, Russell," she said, quickly moving a little to the side, so that his hand fell away. "I've seen the photo on your desk," she murmured.

"Oh, that," he said, almost as surprised as she was by his bold move. His face reddened. "My wife and I are presently separated," he added, as if that justified his making a move. While technically, he was correct that they were separated. But he didn't bother to explain that this was a temporary arrangement, that his wife was in Mt. Vernon caring for her parents, and it had nothing to do with any apparent problems in their marriage; although such problems were now making themselves known to Russell.

"I'm sorry to hear that," replied Candi, feeling a sense of confusion. This consultation was taking a whole new direction for her. True, it was not something she hadn't thought about in the quiet of her bedroom back in town, but still it had always been just something that had been more of a casual fantasy than any notion that it might or could become a reality. It must be the musk, she thought, or the Old Spice, or the Aqua Velva. She reached over and touched the back of his hand and felt him immediately tense up. She felt an urge to console him. After all, he had confessed to a personal tragedy, had taken her into his confidence. It was all so different from her encounters at the bar, where she felt nothing. Or her life with Jesse, when she felt little more than rage.

Russell moved even closer. Then he leaned down and gently kissed the nape of her neck. The notebook of poems fell to the ground. Poetry and Christian literature were now suddenly the last things on her mind - or his.

CHAPTER 29

THAT EVENING JESSE AND BIG CAL FOUND THEIR WAY BACK TO THE Round 'em Up for an evening of hamburgers, beer drinking and pool. There had been no sign of Candi at the conference center while they were lurking around, scouting out the facilities. Jesse wasn't even certain what their next step should be. He was sure she was there somewhere but he didn't just want to approach someone and ask. He was afraid of what her reaction might be if she knew he was around, following her. She had been pretty pissed the last time he had talked with her on the phone. In person she might really explode. For such a delicate looking creature, she could be a pistol when it counted. Big Cal had no idea why they were really here and simply did whatever Jesse said to do. Tonight it was the Round 'em Up. The tavern was just several blocks off the main drag, away from the artsy, touristy parts of town. It was a one-story wooden building, made to look like a ranch bunkhouse, with a huge neon sign over the door blinking red and green of a cowboy riding on his bucking bronco, holding on for dear life, his hat in his hand, waving up and down. A place for the locals to hang out.

Jesse bent low over the pool table and eyed a corner shot. "Eight ball in the far corner pocket," he announced, as he lined it up.

Cal stood off to one side, leaning on his pool cue, a bottle of Bud in his hand. The Round 'em Up was busy. Both pool tables were occupied; the big plasma television set up on the wall in one corner was blaring out the play by play of a Mariner's baseball game from Seattle; the jukebox was wailing with country-western

106

music, and gaudy beer signs blinked on and off behind the bar. Ichiro had just hit a double with two men on base, who scored easily and the crowd at Safeco Field was going mad. It was the bottom of the eighth.

This was Cal and Jesse's second night entertaining themselves here and even the bartender, who told them her name was Gloria, had started treating them like regulars. She was a little leery of Big Cal, but Jesse looked as though he could fit right into Wallowa County life pretty well. In fact Gloria was thinking he might fit into anything she had pretty well. Jesse had asked what her last name was the first night and when she told him "Springwater," (which she said was an Indian name) he immediately had made the claim to her that he too was Native American. Nez Perce, he had said, although he looked more Italian to her than Indian, given his dark, curly hair. But she realized that looks weren't everything in the Native American world. She herself had grown up on the Umatilla Reservation outside of Pendleton.

"Yeah," Jesse had said, "My People (he always referred to them as 'My People') go way back. Hundreds and hundreds of years. We used to own these parts." He gestured toward the mountains. "Until the while man fucked us over." He thought using terms like "these parts" made him sound like a local.

Gloria had been working at the Round 'em Up for about two years. She had dropped out of her second year of high school while living on the reservation, and bummed around the Pendleton area for some time, working at odd jobs in convenience stores and gas stations. Then, when she was about twenty she hooked up with a young guy she knew from the reservation named Clyde Running Horse, and eventually followed him here to Joseph, where he had found work as a ranch hand, on this far side of the state and the beginning to nowhere. And it was the beginning of nowhere. Clyde, it turned out, was more interested in beer, drugs and other women than he was in Gloria, and she finally realized that, after two black eyes, a broken rib and a couple of trips to the emergency room over in Enterprise, followed by the need for a restraining order, they were never going to make it as a couple. By then they had a child, Raymond, who was now three years old. She had decided to bail. So, now in her mid-twenties Gloria took this job at the Round 'em Up and had been keeping the customers, mostly local ranch hands, in check ever since. She had become an institution here now and took shit from no man. She was clearly in charge. And working here in the Round 'em Up she had seen it all. Or thought she had. Except for the likes of Big Cal. She'd never seen anybody, or anything quite like Big Cal before. Most of the ranch boys were grizzled and gnarled and skinny and just bone and muscle. Big Cal was big, and thick. From any angle. He looked like a walking retaining wall, she thought when she'd first laid eyes on him. From the moment he had entered the tavern he had seemed to fill it with his bulk. But still he seemed harmless enough. In his dumb ox way, he was kind of cute. Kind of cuddly. And he said little and was always polite to her, something that was not always the case with the other customers. Jesse, however, was someone, Indian or not, she could relate to. Aside from having a serious twitch that seemed to jump off of his face uncontrollably at times, he was a looker.

"What are you fellas doin' in town," Gloria asked, sliding another beer across to Cal?

"We're here to check out the conference over at the lake," said Jesse. "You know anything about it?"

"Yeah, some sort of writers' thing. Religious nuts." Gloria turned to the cash register and rang up Jesse's tab. "They're here every summer. And sometimes for a couple of weeks in the winter too." She paused and wiped down the bar with a damp towel. "We don't see much of 'em in here though." She paused again. "Except for a few who kinda sneak in here and drink on the sly. Evil, you know." She laughed. "One of 'em, a big, fat guy, always wearing a loud checked suit, tried to grab my ass just the other night when I took an order to his table. I told him if he tried that again he'd be in the E.R., and they'd be operating to pull a beer bottle out of his ass." She laughed at her own story. "You guys involved with that?" They didn't look the part, she thought.

"Nah," said Jesse. "We've got a friend who is part of it. We just came up to check it out." He glanced up at the big screen TV. Ken Griffey, Jr. had just struck out in the bottom of the nineth and the Mariners had lost again. Safeco Field had gone quiet.

"I read in the paper that they've got some big names over there from the literary world. If anybody's interested, that is. Some guy all the way from Russia who won more than a million dollars for his writing. Got a big international prize and all that money. A fuckin' Russian with all that money." Gloria looked wistful as she lit a cigarette and blew out the match. "I think I read where he's giving some sort of reading over there tomorrow night. They said locals are welcome. Free of charge."

"Shit," said Cal, opening his big mouth for the first time. He was a little intimidated by Gloria. "That's a bundle. And just for doin' some writing." He stared down at his beer bottle, drawing circles in the moisture that had formed on the bar. "Don't make much sense." He was wondering if a guy like that had ever been on the Larry Singer Show. If he had, he'd missed the episode.

"Some Russian guy, you say," said Jesse. He looked thoughtful, which for Jesse wasn't all that easy. "It's too fuckin' bad when some asshole from another country gets that kind of money. Especially some Russian." He paused to watch the last of the crowd trail out of Safeco Field and the announcers were wrapping up the game and interviewing the losing Seattle manager. "What the hell do they ever do for our people?" He looked inquiringly at Gloria. "They don't do shit for our people." By "our people," of course, he meant himself and his Indian comrades.

Gloria went on swabbing down the bar and nodded. "Yeah, they don't do much for us." She turned and tossed the wet towel into the sink. "Maybe he'll remember me in his Will," she said, laughing.

"Maybe he should remember all of us," mused Jesse. "Maybe he should," his right cheek suddenly started twitching furiously.

Jesse sat quietly for a few more minutes, absorbing the atmosphere of the bar and the beer, and watching Gloria as she moved
easily from table to table, keeping the boys happy. A million bucks,
he thought. More than a million bucks. Just sittin' on the other
side of the lake, not more than six miles away. Six miles from where
the two of them, he and Big Cal, sat broke and sleepin' in a shithole
motel. He had never in his life been that close to that much money.
He'd buy himself the biggest, most expensive 4 X 4 pick-up truck
money could buy. He could not even imagine what it would be like
to have that kind of money. But, he thought, he'd sure like to find
out. He surely would.

CHAPTER 30

CANDI WOKE TO THE SOUNDS OF BIRDS IN THE TREES JUST OUTSIDE THE yurt and the sunlight pouring in through the dusty windows. It was early and Nell and the others were still sleeping. She had not slept well herself. For the longest time she had lain awake, tossing and turning. Finally she had fallen into a troubled and restless sleep. And now she crept down from her upper bunk, pulled on some clothes, made a futile effort to fix up her hair a bit and quietly left the yurt and, with her notebook of poems in hand, walked down through the forest to the old Wallowa Lake Lodge, where she sat in the early morning sun on one of the wooden deck chairs on the wide expanse of lawn and watched the lake coming to life.

Yes, Candi had had a troubled night. Her encounter with Russell Kees the previous afternoon had left her with feelings of confusion. She knew she had been drawn to him before, but had never viewed those feelings as anything other than a student crush on a professor that had no sense of reality. That was no longer the case. Despite her early history with Pastor Bob, and what some might consider her tawdry work at the strip club, and despite her time with Jesse, she had never really been in love before. She had never felt that overwhelming sense of attraction, that desire to simply be with another person. She had learned at an early age, thanks to Pastor Bob, how to simply use her body as a means of advancing herself to one degree or another. But what she was feeling now was very different. Suddenly she was no longer as interested in writing poems to the glory of God, as she was to the glory of Love, to the mutual physical and emotional attraction of one person to another. In this case, of a particular woman for a particular man. The direction of the conference was shifting under her feet. She flipped open her notebook to a blank page and, in a long flowing hand, began to write.

Meanwhile Russell had also had difficulty sleeping. He had been reading a book Viktor had brought with him, *The Power of the Moment*. He had seen Zuber on the Winfrey show. In addition to the fact that Viktor sounded like he was reenacting World War II, for a long time Russell had simply lain there thinking over the events of the afternoon. Wife Lucy had quickly retreated to the further most recesses of his mind and memory. She was off in Mt. Vernon, off tending the old folks, far from home. That was another world, or so it seemed. And he was here, in the setting of this lovely wilderness, alone. Well, not so alone anymore. Candi had been responsive to him. He wanted her. It was as simple as that. In his heart of hearts he knew something was profoundly wrong with all that but he was helpless to rationalize his feelings. He knew he was a romantic at heart, a poet, after all. He simply wanted her.

Also Russell was beginning to recognize that he was no longer as young as he had once been. When he looked in the mirror each morning to shave he could see the sags beginning to form in his face, the lids of the eyes that looked back at him beginning to droop; what had once been fairly decent pecs were beginning to navigate south to where his stomach was supposed to be hard and flat. And, of course, there was the growing bald spot on the crown of his head that he had recently covered with a hairpiece purchased through a TV advertisement. He had to admit to himself that he was flattered by Candi's apparent interest in him. He knew that with her looks and youth, she could attract most any man on the planet. At least any man within a twenty-mile radius of East Hills Liberty College. He had watched that night at Nockers' Up-town Bar and Grille as the men crowded around the stage, lunging for her, thrusting bills into what was left of her clothing. While she danced for them, she never seemed to be expressing any real interest in them. Even the cops who hung around the bar like magnets. But she had expressed an interest in him. Their mutual needs appeared to be suddenly colliding. He could not deny that somewhere deep down, he had hoped for this development. But he had not really expected it.

Finally Russell rose from his bed with Viktor still asleep and roaring away in the other bedroom, the windows shuddering with his snores. Quietly he made a pot of coffee, poured a cup and walked out onto the front porch. He sat down on the steps and watched while three inquisitive deer, two does and a half-grown fawn, came skittering out of the trees and stared at him, begging for something to eat. Lazy buggers, he thought. The forest is full of food for them. He had nothing for them and they soon gave up and disappeared back into the heavy underbrush and dense canopy of trees. He thought of his comfortable but rather boring life back in town, his comfortable but often boring position at East Hills Liberty College, with its strict code of conduct, so often violated by teachers consorting with their students. He thought of his home and all that would now be in jeopardy by the confusion he felt, and what would happen if he just followed his heart. And, of course, there was his dick that was entering into the equation. This nubile young woman had entered his life now as something more than just a student, or even as a stripper at a local bar. She was flesh and blood. She was real. He had kissed her neck. She had responded. In some tangible way, on some physical level, he thought she could be his.

BIG CAL LAY BY THE MOTEL SWIMMING POOL, SWEATING, AND HUGE AS a beached beluga whale, while Jesse was taking a quick dip in the cooling waters. It was already getting hot, the chill of early morning having dissipated. The sun had risen above the mountains to the east and was a solid, yellow ball stuck against a clear blue sky. But the beauty of it all was lost on Big Cal. He was just enjoying the swimming pool and the fact that he wasn't at work at the club or stuck in his trailer. And the motel. It was all more luxury than he could ever remember having experienced before in his entire life. The motel, the swimming pool, the ice dispensers at the end of each wing of the building, the coke machines. There was even a beer fridge in the room. And a coffee pot and a microwave oven. No, he had never had it so good. He was wondering if he could ever go back to the meagerness of trailer park living again after all this. He looked around and surveyed the placid scene before him. Life was lookin' good to him. He was still concerned about the where-abouts of Candi, and worried that she might need his help, but he was finally beginning to simply relax and space out, and go with the flow of the good life here in Joseph. This is what a vacation is supposed to be, he thought. He had never had a real vacation before. He'd been laid off before. Fired before. But he'd never been on vacation before. He watched as Jesse took an awkward dive off the spring board, his long, dark hair running slick down his back. Big Cal would never try that, he thought. He didn't even like to take baths all that much. Jesse knifed his way through the water, his arm flailing frantically, to the edge of the pool, pulled himself up and yelled to Cal.

"Hey, Big Fella, get me a beer."

Cal nodded, pulled himself up from the chaise lounge and ambled back to the room where he got four cold cans of Schlitz out of the fridge and brought them back to the pool, along with a giant bag of Fritos chips. Yes, life was good. He and Jesse appeared to be the only occupants still registered at the motel that morning, as best he could tell. The parking lot was virtually empty of cars. The "Vacancy" sign was lit and blinking off and on. The old Honda was one of the few cars still in the guest parking lot, just sitting there with transmission fluid oozing out from underneath it, except for a newer pick-up truck. That apparently belonged to either the desk clerk or the day manager, and also a battered white Chevy mini-van that had been used to bring the room maids to the motel for their day's work. A couple of the maids looked pretty damned good to Big Cal. He opened a beer and handed it down to Jesse, who was now lolling at the edge of the pool, and then he opened one for himself. He eased his over-heated bulk slowly back into the chaise lounge and lay back. Yes, life was good. He sucked at his can of beer. Jesse pulled himself out of the pool, toweled off and sat down in the lounge chair next to him. The high mountain air contained a slight breeze that felt good. The two of them tapped their beer cans together and raised them in a salute to each other.

"God Damn, Big Fella, ain't this the good life, though?" Jesse looked over at Cal and again raised his beer to him. "If we had the freakin' bucks, we could live like this all the time."

Cal turned that over in his mind. The same thought had occurred to him, but more slowly. He hadn't really put it into words before. "Yeah, if we had the bucks," he muttered. "But we don't." He watched as one of the motel maids tripped her way across the walkway with a load of fresh towels in her arms, her ample hips swaying provocatively, her dark hair caught up behind her in a ponytail, swinging back and forth to the rhythm of her work.

"We could," said Jesse, staring off straight ahead toward the mountains that loomed over them in the distance to the south, rising above the lake. He looked over at Big Cal and smiled his best Jesse Red Hawk smile

"I been thinkin', you know, about that fuckin' Russian prick over at the conference." He paused. "You know, the one with a million bucks or more in his pocket. Can you imagine? A million bucks! When he won that big prize? And for what? He wrote somethin'. As if anybody who really wanted to couldn't do that. It's not like winnin' the lottery or somethin' important like that." He paused again and turned to look directly at Cal, whose broad face displayed all the expression of a blank wall. "It just pisses me off that some foreign asshole has that kind of money and you and me, real Americans, and me even more than you, being Indian and all, and here we are, out of work, like me, or doin' some shit-hole job like you got."

Cal wasn't so sure where Jesse was going with this. His job wasn't that bad. He got to see all the girls in the backroom, which was off limits to anyone who didn't work there, he got paid for it too and he occasionally got a share of the tip money from the girls - at least from Candi - and he could eat all the microwave bar food he wanted. "So, what's it to us?" Cal asked. He was vainly trying to make some sort of connection to what Jesse was getting at, but it wasn't coming through to him. "Why don't we just play the lottery? Maybe we'd win a million dollars. I've heard of folks who did."

Jesse looked at him and sneered. "Better yet, we could just take some of his." Jesse looked past Cal at the room maid now retracing her steps back toward the front office, slowly pushing her supply cart.

"What you gettin' at? Like rob the prick?" Cal asked. He laughed at what he thought was a joke. He could just see the two of them sticking a gun in the old fart's ribs and taking his money. Then he thought it over for a few minutes. "Do you think he's got it on him?"

Jesse practically barfed up his beer. "Course not, stupid. He doesn't carry it around in his pocket. It's in a bank somewheres. Probably one of those Swiss banks that nobody knows about. He probably doesn't even pay taxes on it, like a good American would." Jesse had never knowingly paid a cent of tax in his life.

Big Cal was having some difficulty keeping up with Jesse on this one, but he didn't like being call "stupid," even if he knew he was. All the insults from his youth stirred in him. He stared hard at Jesse, stood and drew himself up to full height and width. Since he almost blotted out the sun, his actions were not lost on Jesse, who backed away slightly. "So, you thinkin' of asking him for some of it?" asked Cal. "A loan, or somethin' like that?"

"Not a loan." Jesse was going to call him "stupid" again, but thought better of it. "Look, we just happen to take the old bastard for a little hike up into those mountains and hang on to him for a while until he's ready for a pay-off. He comes up with some real cash and he gets to go home. Otherwise, we just keep him up there in the mountains." He pointed to the south. Then he took up a baggie of good grass from his shirt pocket that was lying on the metal table placed between the lounge chairs, slowly rolled a joint and lit up. With that he got up and began pacing back and forth for several minutes, the smoke trailing after him, letting his remarks get through Cal's thick skull. "I'll bet a few days up there eating pinecones and deer shit, and he'd be more than glad to shake loose of a half mill or so." He leaned over and blew a cloud of smoke in Cal's face. That was a mistake. For all his faults, Cal didn't often do drugs. "Call it a gift," Jesse laughed. "And it would be tax free, too. No one would even know we had it. We could move to Belize or someplace down in the Caribbean and live like kings. We could live like this." He gestured at the motel swimming pool. "Only better. Booze. Crank. Pussy. You name it. We could have it. All of it."

Big Cal relaxed a bit, and sat back down. He looked dubious, however. But then, Big Cal looked dubious most of the time. Still, he was having trouble tracking Jesse on this one especially. Finally it sunk in. The light bulb lit up above his massive head. "What if we get caught?" He felt a sense of pride at having spotted the weakness in Jesse's idea so quickly.

"How could we get caught?" asked Jesse. "For one thing, who'd ever miss an old geezer like that? I doubt he's even got any family around here. There's nobody to miss him. We just pick him up as he's wandering away from the campground by himself. He won't give us any shit. He's too old to put up a fuss. And think of this, if it's true he has no next of kin (Jesse felt good that he could use such a term as "next of kin; Big Cal was clearly impressed). When the old guy kicks off, there'll be no one left to inherit his money anyway. We'd be doin' him a favor by relieving him of some of it." He laughed at his own joke and the brilliance of his logic. Big Cal was still trying to put two and two together. It wasn't working. He slowly lifted his left buttock and let out a soft rumble, the result of the beer settling down into his massive digestive track and a touch of gas from the bean burritos he'd had at the 711 store for breakfast.

Jesse moved back a notch as the foul odor passed by. The hang time was impressive. "Think what you could do and buy with a quarter million dollars rattlin' around in your pocket." The cute motel maid had now been joined by another maid and they were on a break, enjoying a cigarette and strolling across the walkway on the other side of the pool, glancing shyly over at Jesse and giggling slightly. "You could even have all of that you wanted," said Jesse, pointing with his beer can to the girls. "They'd go down on you in a fuckin' New York minute if you had that kind of cash." He paused to watch the girls drift off toward the supply room. "Just like Hulk Hogan."

The mention of Hulk Hogan, another of Cal's heroes, got his full attention. Cal watched the girls as they turned the corner at the end of the building and imagined one of them, either of them, being his very own girl friend. He had never really had a girl friend before. He was certain it was his lack of money that kept them away from him. Even Candi might want him if he had that kind of dough. He would treat her right too, and she might even go to

Hollywood with him and they could get tickets to the Larry Singer Show. He'd protect her for the rest of her life, he thought.

"So, what do we do?" Cal wanted to know.

"We keep an eye out for him," Jesse answered. "He should be easy to spot. And when we see him off by himself somewhere, we take him for a little ride up into those mountains, up there to a trailhead I saw on a map in the front office. Those maps have a lot of information on hiking and backpacking into the wilderness areas. So we hike him from the trailhead into the wilderness, and camp out with him until he agrees to give us the numbers to his bank account. I'm told there's a little hut up there for skiers in the wintertime and we can use that if we can find it. Once he gives us what we need to raid his bank accounts I'll hike back to the car, ride into town and arrange to get the money. When I have it all taken care of I'll call you on your cell phone and you can come back down too. I'll pick you up at the trailhead."

"What about the old Russian?" asked Cal.

"Just leave him up there. He can find his own way back." Jesse chuckled at the thought.

"What if he don't make it?"

"Tough shit. That's his problem, not ours." Jesse smiled. "If he doesn't make it out, when they find him they'll just think he went up there by himself and didn't know what he was doin' and croaked." He paused. "We Indians know our way around. If the old white guy doesn't, that too fuckin' bad."

"But I'm not an Indian either," protested Cal. "What if I don't make it back?" Then another thought struck him. "What if you just take the money and head off to some place down south, Belle Air, or whatever it is." He tended to stutter sometimes when he didn't know quite what to say.

"Belize. And don't worry, my man. If you can't trust me, who can you trust?" He grinned. "Besides, my unemployment money's about to run out. And you don't make jack-shit at that titty bar. What you got to lose?"

Cal took some time thinking this over. It was clear that Jesse had been thinking about this for some time. He had even done some checking out of the trails and of the hut up on the mountain. He seemed to know what he was doing. And he was a Nez Perce after all. But after all was said and done, there were some benefits to working at the bar. He got to see a lot of bare flesh, even if he couldn't touch it. And he got paid, however little. That was a lot better than some guys ever got. It was certainly better than nothing. Far better than ending up in jail. Or worse.

"Do you really know your way around up there?" Cal pointed toward the perpetually snow-capped peaks of the Wallowas looming in the distance, cold and dispassionate. "I've never been up in a wilderness before."

"Man, this is my country. Nez Perce. Remember? This where my people lived for centuries until you white bastards ran 'em out. The wilderness is in my blood." Jesse puffed out his chest and thumped it a bit. He did a little war dance for the benefit of the motel maids. They only laughed.

"Well, maybe we could just scare the shit out of him a little bit, and he'd just give us the money, without having to take him into the wilderness." Cal was beginning to get with the flow of the idea, even though he wasn't thrilled by the specifics as Jesse was outlining them. He could certainly use a quarter of a million dollars. He had to admit that.

The motel girls across the way had finished their cigarette break and were straightening the lounge chairs on the other side of the pool and were still glancing over their shoulders at them from time to time. While Cal knew he could always just go back to the strip club, he also knew he would still just be part of the furniture, no better than a table or a chair or an oversized sofa. He'd never have a girl like that little chubby gal who was smiling shyly at him from across the pool. Jesse's plan was beginning to take hold in his dim brain. He decided that his future demanded action. He was tired of being just big, dumb Cal. This was his chance to be something more.

"So, how do we do it?" he asked. He stared at the girls across the way. He was certain that little fat one had winked at him. She wants me, he thought. She must think I'm rich.

CHAPTER 32

PASTOR BOB FAIRLY, IN HIS OFFICIAL ROLE AS CONFERENCE CHAPLAIN, was supposed to be spending most of his time preparing the daily devotional services. One took place first thing in the morning, complete with an inspirational message to get the conferees into their day. Then there was a brief prayer session at lunch, and finally an evening vesper service, following the evening events, readings and lectures, complete with hymns of praise and testimonials from believers and new converts, all attesting to how Jesus had come into their lives and saved them from eternal damnation. Pastor Bob had noticed that not everyone was staying for the evening service, although they were supposed to, and he was about to report his concerns to Redd Benson. He was also available to counsel with those who might be inclined to stray from the Word of God and be lured into sinful activity. It was his accustomed routine to wander about the conference grounds in the evening, after all the activities had been done for the day, watching for any signs of behavior suggestive of sin, a couple sitting too close to one another on the boat dock, those furtive glances between participants across the dinner table, a style of dress that seemed unusually gaudy or prurient. If he saw any such deviations from what was expected to be the norm at God+Write, it was his duty, he felt, to intervene and bring the malefactors back into the fold of the Godly. And who better than Pastor Bob, after all, to recognize sin in all its manifestations?

On this particular evening as he was wandering down by the lake, keeping an ever vigilant eye out for such naughtiness, he spied

Viktor Karshenko sitting by himself on a large rock that protruded from the shoreline, just where the icy-cold waters of the rampaging Wallowa River burst down the mountainside and spilled into the lake. The sun had disappeared some time ago behind the line of mountains and the shore was now bathed in deepening shadow. It was getting chilly and Pastor Bob pulled the jacket of his favorite leisure suit closer around his ample middle. Despite his years of working in small churches in rural communities in eastern Oregon, and his brief time earlier at Wallowa Lake working for the church camp, he had never become really an "outdoorsy sort of guy," in any sense. He was at heart a town boy. Not a city boy, but a town boy. His tasseled highly shined wing-tipped loafers were not the best shoes for this more rugged terrain but they were all he had. He was probably the only man in eastern Oregon still wearing calf-high silk socks held up by garters. But it was just who he was. His style, if you like. He wasn't about to change his wardrobe just to please the more rough and tumble crowd here at the conference. In this crowd, with everybody else looking like they'd been dressed by REI or L.L. Bean, he was going to maintain a certain sense of dignity, a certain sense of decorum, a certain professionalism.

And so he stumbled his way through the brush and tall grasses to the rock where Viktor Karshenko was sitting, contemplating the brilliance of the universe that shone down from the distant black sky overhead, vivid with stars. Pastor Bob had met Viktor only briefly at the orientation, and had not had an opportunity to really chat with him. He had serious doubts about Viktor, however. There was some scuttlebutt about the fact that the old man was a Jew, and not a Christian, and that he had - bless his soul - nonetheless won some huge amount of money. It didn't seem quite right to Pastor Bob that God should reward a Jew with such handsome winnings and for him to now have so much money, when there were so many good and godly Christians (he had himself in mind, in particular) who could have used all that cash for much better purposes. Thus he felt somewhat conflicted about Viktor.

Pastor Bob liked the idea of a lot of money, even if he didn't like the idea of a Jew having all that much of it. Like many of his fellow pastors, he was irristiably attracted to the lure of dollars. After all, the Good Book made it clear that wealth was not something to be avoided. It spoke of tithing and God getting his ten percent (a most reasonable amount, not much more than the amount a realtor might expect) and ten percent of one million dollars and more, which Karshenko was reported to have received, was still a quite handsome sum by anybody's calculations. And Pastor Bob had developed the knack over the years of making such calculations quickly in his head, although he had never had the opportunity to make such a generous calculation. He could be a veritable electronic calculator if the circumstances called for it. And these circumstances clearly called for it. Perhaps, if properly motivated, Viktor Karshenko could be persuaded to participate in a generous division of his purported wealth. He might even be made to feel that ten percent was far too little an offering to make toward the furthering of Pastor Bob's good works. After all, didn't Jews read the Good Book too? Or at least the Old Testament, which was really Pastor Bob's favorite book, with all that killing and wrath and fire and brimstone. Yes, he loved it. That and, of course, then there was the book of Revelations. Who better to receive the benefits of such generosity than Pastor Bob? Opportunity lay before him like an aging Jew on a rock.

"Evenin', Mr. Karshenko," said Pastor Bob, in his best Pastor Bob tone of voice, the low bass sounds rumbling lovingly on the ear. "Nice night for contemplating the wonders of the Almighty."

Viktor turned and looked up at Bob, then rose to his feet and approached him with his hand outstretched.

"Pashtor Fairly, I believe? Sho gald to shee you again." He sat back down and scooted over to make room for Pastor Bob's more than generous backside. Pastor Bob cleared away some lichen that had attached itself to the rock and settled his portly frame next to Viktor. "Nishh evening, no?" said Viktor, looking out over the lake as two mallard ducks, frightened by a deer that had come to the water's edge to drink, came frantically winging out of the shadows. The birds came in for a landing just off shore, small waves breaking from beneath their feathered chests as they skimmed onto the surface of the lake.

"Mr. Karshenko, I understand you are from Russia," said Pastor Bob. "I've always been fascinated by Russian history." He paused dramatically. He knew absolutely nothing about Russian history, except that Stalin had been one mean guy. "I've been doing some research lately into conditions in Russia before the revolution."

"Ah," muttered Viktor. "The revolution. Itsh a bloody history. Three hundred years of Romanov rule, followed by the Communist takeover." He shook his head in disgust.

"Yes," said Pastor Bob. "Those damned Godless communists." He nodded his head up and down in agreement. "I'd be thrilled if we could get together from time to time while we're both here and you could tell me more about your life in Russia, about struggling to be a free man and finally having the opportunity of living here in the United States of America in freedom. Yes, freedom here in the good old U.S. of A." His voice rose and fell as if he were suddenly preaching to the masses. He looked Viktor in the face and smiled. "And you have been so well rewarded for your struggles and your constant pursuit of democracy."

"Well, yesh," said Viktor, looking a bit puzzled. He was flattered that this man of the cloth (the cloth, in this case, being a rather loud checked leisure suit) was interested in what he might have to say about conditions in Russia, or his efforts to come to this country. Everyone was making him feel so welcome out here in Oregon. It certainly seemed like God's Country, all right. Just like the guidebooks had said. He'd have to think of some nice way to reciprocate. Perhaps a small kickback of some of his expense money would be appropriate, a small donation to the work of the mission fund for abused puppies in Thailand that Pastor Fairly had so eloquently described just last night at the evening services. While

Viktor had not been too excited about the condition in his contract stipulating that he would attend some of those religious functions, he had done so with a sense of good will and he felt it was the least he could do to respond to the generous souls, even if the endless praying and supplicating and loud singing at the drop of a hat was starting to get on his nerves a bit. It may not be teaching at Harvard or Yale. Or even Robarts, for that matter. But still he felt a certain sense of contentment, here on the shores of this lovely, idyllic lake. Perhaps a check for fifty dollars would be appropriate. And, he had been told, it would be tax-deductable. Viktor felt Pastor Bob's chubby right arm circle around him, clutch at his shoulder and give him a friendly squeeze. Yes, he was beginning to feel quite at home here. The welcome had been extraordinary.

"Shall we pray?" Pastor Bob bowed his head, visions of Viktor's ten percent dancing in his head.

CHAPTER 33

THE ROUND 'EM UP BAR WAS UNUSUALLY QUIET WHEN JESSE AND CAL came in that evening. It was early and hardly anybody was there. No one was at the pool tables, and only a disreputable looking pair of down-at the-heels cowboys lurked at the far end of the bar, the air surrounding them cloudy with cigarette smoke and bullshit. Gloria was working behind the bar, as usual, wiping it down when they took stools at the opposite end from the cowboys. Jesse lit up, passed his cigarettes to Cal and he too lit up.

"Well, if it ain't the Big City boys, back again," Gloria said, with a slightly sarcastic smile on her face. "What'll ya have?"

"Couple of drafts," said Jesse, blowing a perfect smoke ring her way. She immediately poked at it and it dispersed. Cal nodded his approval of the order.

"Comin' right up." Gloria held the tall, chilled glasses to the tap and drew two beers, letting the heads settle for a moment, and then set them down in front of the two men. Jesse handed her a ten dollar bill and she quickly made change and put what was left on the bar. She hoped for a tip, but knew the likelihood was not great.

"You fellas plannin' on movin' here to Joseph?" She paused and then looked down at the two cowboys at the other end of the bar and smiled. "We could always use a few extra hands around here." She laughed, and the cowboys laughed too. In fact Gloria could not remember seeing two more unlikely candidates for cowboys. Jesse might say he was an Indian, but he looked a hell of a lot softer than most men around here. And Cal - shit, he'd kill a horse if he ever climbed on one.

"You're lookin' good tonight, Gloria," said Jesse, slurping the head off his beer. "How do you do it, night after night?" He was staring boldly at her generous bust line. "What's your secret?"

"I got my rodeo bra on tonight," she whispered in a voice loud enough to be heard by the good old boys at the other end of the bar.

"How's that work?" asked Cal, also now staring down at her magnificent chest.

"It rounds 'em up and moves 'em out." Gloria laughed loudly at her own joke and turned to look at her monumental profile in the mirror behind the bar. She had told that one before.

The cowboys let out a loud guffaw, then got up and headed for one of the pool tables. "Show 'em a couple of pointers, Gloria," called out one of them, as they selected cues and set up the balls. One of the cowboys stuck the end of the pool cue into his tight jeans and showed the sharp bulge to Gloria. "Better get over here and take care of this," he called out. The other cowboy laughed as if this were the funniest thing he'd ever seen.

"Go fuck yourself," yelled Gloria right back, and turned away, feigning disgust.

"You fellas lookin' for work around here or just up to no good."

Jesse grinned. "We're just up to no good." he said, as he reached over and plucked a pickled sausage from the tall jar that sat on the bar in front of him and bit off a spicy chunk. Gloria took some more money from the stack of change to pay for it. "What do you know about that wilderness area up above the lake?" he asked, pointing to the south and chewing heartily.

"The Eagle Cap Wilderness?" she said, a serious look drifted across her broad, dark face. These boys didn't look like hikers and backpackers to her. "If you're plannin' on goin' up there you'd better take a guide. Somebody who knows what the hell he's doin'. Folks get lost up there all the time. Most of the time they aren't equipped for it. Even in summer, it's cold there."

"What kind of gear should they have?" asked Cal, eyeing Jesse as the remains of his sausage disappeared into his mouth. He liked the word "gear." He thought it made him sound as if he knew what he was talking about.

"Even in summer." Gloria continued, "it's colder'n shittin' in an outhouse in Alaska in winter up there. Snow deeper'n your asshole in some places. You'd need a good tent, good Gore-Tex clothing, a gun, food, water, stove, first-aid stuff. Everything for survival."

Gloria drew two more beers for the cowboys still playing pool, put them on a tray and carried it over to them. The front door opened and another customer came in, an older man who walked with a cane and had a long ponytail of gray hair running down his back. He sat down at the other end of the bar, where the cowboys had been sitting earlier. Gloria greeted him and went down to take his order.

"Shit," said Cal. "This don't sound so great."

Jesse smirked. "That's cause you ain't an Indian, Cal." He looked at his reflection in the bar mirror, turned slightly to the side to see his profile and shook his dark hair across his shoulders, enjoying the view. "If you're an Indian, it don't bother you none."

"Sides, we ain't even got a gun, let alone any of the rest of that crap.," Cal noted accurately. "And we ain't got much money left, either." Gordie Nockers had reluctantly given him an advance of his pay check, and that was almost gone. Cal knew Jesse had some money from his latest unemployment check, but that must be almost gone by now too.

"We can get a gun easy, and all the rest of what we need easy." Jesse said. "I saw a gun show being advertized when we were comin' through that town of Enterprise on our way up here. We could go back tomorrow and pick up somethin'. The rest we can get at the Walmart right outside of town. And we got that credit card we can use."

Big Cal, in his slow mind, was beginning to rethink this entire venture. It had been great sitting by the pool this afternoon, enjoying the sun and the pool and watching the roommaids wiggle their asses at them and bullshit about big money. But this didn't sound that great. Hiking up into the wilderness, even in summer, was not his idea of fun. He was quick when he needed to toss some prick out of the bar, but he wasn't sure he was up to a long trek in the woods.

But then, as the jukebox roared into life with the latest hits from Nashville blaring and, with another beer under his belt, he slowly began to relax again. He watched closely as Gloria bent down over the refrigerator getting out a cold bottle of beer for the newcomer, her broad rear-end stuck up in the air, the cheeks of her ass straining against the denim of her pants, tantalizing him. Maybe it wasn't such a bad idea after all, he thought. Maybe Jesse was right. Maybe this was really his golden opportunity to make something of himself. Maybe this was his chance to strike it rich and maybe then Candi would see him in a new light. He was sure he would never be this close to a real, live millionaire again in his life. The more he thought about it, the more he was sure he would really like to be rich, lyin' on that sunny beach somewhere in the Caribbean, and maybe with Candi jumpin' all over his body. Or, better yet, the two of them appearing as guests on the Larry Singer Show. Right there in sunny Southern California. Good Old Hollywood. The crowd cheering them on. He could just see it now. The two of them together for life. TV stars. "Oh, Cal, I love you," she'd be saying. "Do me again, you big hunk."

CHAPTER 34

THE FIRST WEEK OF GOD+WRITE SEEMED TO GO BY IN QUICKLY FOR everyone involved. The workshops, readings and socializing were enjoyed by all. Beginning Friday night and through the weekend there were plans for all sorts of special activities, activities intended to extend well beyond the conferees themselves. Members of the community as well as supporters from all around the region were invited in to participate, much like a fundamentalist's form of Woodstock, with Christian rock bands, like "Fire and Brimstone," whose hit on the Christian Hit Parade, "Rock it to Me, Jesus", made it to number one for almost six months the year before. There were more readings, now by invited guests from outside the conference, as well as a potluck dinner on Saturday night, and, of course, a gigantic "Praise the Lord" Service on Sunday morning, held outdoors, in a large, open space near the lake, which included not only Pastor Bob Fairly and the former Rev. Redd Benson, but also an evangelist from Laguna Beach, California, Brother Antonio Roach, whose approach to the Gospel was that wealth was within the reach of everyone - if they just donated enough money to him and his ministry. He was also willing to accept donations in kind, such as BMWs and vacation homes. Thus far Brother Roach had been highly successful and his offerings of a small vial of holy water, free of charge to anyone who displayed sufficient generosity, were well known, especially to the F.B.I., which, unbeknownst to Antonio, was secretly video-taping him at all times, even when he was holed up in a motel with some cutie half his age, accepting whatever gifts she might possess. It would be just a matter of time before his house of cards would come tumbling down, and a long prison sentence might well be in the offering. But for now he was the headliner of the morning's festivities.

Candi and Russell, whose surreptitious relationship was budding like the flowers of spring, sat next to each other at each of the functions through the week of fun and holy games. Russell didn't really care about the fun and holy games but he enjoyed sitting next to Candi. Oddly enough, poor Lucy in Mt. Vernon hadn't entered his thoughts now for the past several days, during which he counseled Candi, looked over her efforts at writing poetry, praised poems that were far from praiseworthy, and, in general, enjoyed basking in her charms. She, on the other hand, was enjoying the attentions of this worldly and erudite man who, despite the hair piece, was far removed from the buffoons and jerks she did business with at the club and the likes of Jesse, who was now far from her thoughts.

In the meantime, Jesse and Big Cal were preparing for their escapade involving Viktor. They had been to Enterprise, where Jesse had purchased a pistol at a gun show. Happily, the paperwork he had to complete was minimal - meaning nonexistent - as was any background check, and he was able to get both the weapon, a used and abused Taurus .38, and some hollow-point ammo without difficulty. That he paid for it with a credit card that he had stolen from the wallet of a drunk customer of the Round 'em Up a couple of nights prior had not yet come to light. He figured he'd be long gone by the time anyone was the wiser. Big Cal was none the wiser either. He, as usual, went along for the ride. After acquiring the pistol, they stopped at the Walmart and outfitted themselves with a small pup tent, two backpacks, a small camp stove, canteens, parkas, a first aid kit, and new boots for each of them. The same stolen credit card was used again. Their last stop was the local liquor store, where they bought a fifth of the local Hood River scotch, as well as a fifth of the cheapest vodka they could find. They were now ready for Viktor.

Viktor, however, was doing his best to avoid the fun times that were taking up the weekend. He attended most of the readings, although he disliked what he heard and could understand, which was not much. He skipped the "Praise the Lord" service entirely, preferring to wander away to the far side of the lake, or up the road, past the horse stables, to a trailhead where he could hike up a fairly gentle incline to an area of falls where the river careened down the hillside. It was quiet up there, unlike the conference grounds, and he could sit for hours and contemplate his new life. It was upon his return, late that Sunday evening, that he encountered Jesse and Big Cal. He was ill prepared for what they had in mind.

CHAPTER 35

Sheriff Jon Wain sat in his police cruiser enjoying the Monday lunch special Valu-Meal from Dinty's Burgers, two Doublepounders, medium fries, and a large diet cola, his motor idling quietly. He had gone through the drive-through and was parked in the parking lot of the restaurant, facing the main drag through Enterprise, the county seat of Wallowa County, casually watching the traffic flowing past for speeders and other miscreants. He had no intention of doing anything about speeders or other miscreants if he saw them, but, as a matter of habit, he kept watch. It was his lunch hour, after all.

Sheriff Wain was the head lawman for Wallowa County, having been elected to the office now for two terms. He had a sergeant and three deputies under him, as well as several reserve officers, mostly local good-ol boys, whose chief function was to help out with crowd control at the annual Chief Joseph Days, which were coming up at the end of the month. Things could get a little wild around here at that time. There were always a few fights, mostly over a woman, a lot of drunkenness, and the occasional group of call girls from Portland or Boise coming in to service some of the cowboys. For backup he had the Oregon State Police, who had a branch office in La Grande, about seventy miles away.

Wallowa County was a peaceful county for the most part, with the exception of Chief Joseph Days, and there wasn't much serious crime. Oh, there was the occasional drug bust, some pot was grown in the hills east of Joseph around Imnaha, of course, and certainly there was some domestic violence, as the courts liked to call it, when a local would get too spirited and take a swing at his wife or girlfriend. Those cases usually got patched up once everybody sobered up. And during elk season there would inevitably be some city slicker from out of town who would shoot someone's cow - what the locals called a "slow elk" - which always led to rustling charges, the most serious felony one could commit in Wallowa County. Why, only last season he had nailed a bone-cracker from Portland who had shot one of Joe Oakley's prize heifers when he couldn't get his elk, and was dragging her off when Joe and a bunch of his boys happened along. That back-snapper was lucky to survive the encounter to face trial after Joe and his hands were done with him. It was a good thing Sheriff Wain had happened along or the man might well have been killed. And murder charges around here were considered less serious than rustling. The jury was out all of fifteen minutes. Long enough to pick a foreman and convict the poor bastard. No local attorney would even dare to represent him, and old Judge Bandy had to appoint some Fancy Dan from Pendleton to come over and take it on. The poor lawyer barely made it out of town in one piece, despite the rapid conviction. Around here, trials for rustling were mere formalities.

Yes, Wallowa County was generally a quiet place to be the sheriff. And Sheriff Wain liked that about the job. He had always wanted to be a police officer and had applied to numerous agencies, including the state police. But none would accept him, despite his having completed high school and having an AA degree in Criminal Justice from Blue Mountain Community College. The problem was he didn't meet the physical qualifications required by most of the agencies where he had applied, in that he was only 5' 5" and that was in his cowboy boots and wearing his Stetson. A trim five foot, five inches, but five foot, five inches nonetheless. Most agencies required their recruits to be at least five foot, seven inches. No matter how he tried to stretch himself out, he could never make the cut.

But here, in Wallowa County, he had been elected by the

people and they didn't care that he was short. He'd grown up in Wallowa County, gone to school here, had been the smallest back on the local high school football team, was well-known, and hoped someday to marry a local girl and settle down. Now that he was Sheriff, folks had even taken to calling him "Duke," a moniker he wore with pride. After all, given his name (a gift from his movie-crazed parents) and despite the difference in the spelling, his hero was, indeed, John Wayne, otherwise known to his Hollywood friends as simply "Duke." He had seen every one of Wayne's westerns, time and again, and delighted in pitching his voice in just that John Wayne sort of way. He had even taken to walking with that particular John Wayne swagger, swaying from side to side, his holstered sidearm riding high on his hip, his night stick swinging, as he walked down the street, or up to a car he had just stopped for a traffic offense.

On this particular afternoon Sheriff Wain was enjoying his second Doublepounder when the call came in on the radio. He had forgotten to turn it off. Some guy with a foreign name was missing, and there was some reason to believe he might have been kidnapped from that Christian conference over at the lake. Name was Viktor Karshenko. What the hell kind of a name was that? he wondered, chomping through a dill pickle. Sounds like some kind of Russian spy name. What the shit's he doin' in Wallowa County, he wondered? Being on his lunch break he ignored the call at first, hoping someone else would take it, and not wanting his medium size fries to get cold or his super-size diet cola to go flat. But finally he figured they would keep after him if he didn't respond.

"Yeah, what's goin' on?"

"We just got a 911 call from that nutty group that's occupying the campground over at the lake, some Christian writing conference. One of their instructors has turned up missing. They say they think he might have been kidnapped." There was a long pause, while the radio crackled. "When's the last time we had a kidnapping?"

"Not since I've been Sheriff," answered Duke Wain, his mouth full of Doublepounder, a little catsup running down his chin. Christ Almighty, they put a lot of goop on these things, he thought. He wiped at his chin with his napkin, hoping none of it had dripped down onto his dark brown tie or onto his light tan, recently ironed uniform. Sheriff Wain always prided himself on his appearance while on duty. He had heard of all the attention police officers were supposed to get from the opposite sex, who loved a guy in uniform, and especially one with a pistol at his side, and a long flashlight on his belt, and he always wanted to be ready just in case. So far, it hadn't happened.

"I'm in Enterprise now. Eating lunch." Wain told the dispatcher. " When I'm finished I'll take a run over there and check it out. Maybe you'd best have Harvey come on over too." Harvey was his Sergeant. A big, flabby guy whose stomach inevitably hung far out over his belt, the big buckle lost inside his girth, giving him a perpetually sloppy, unmade-bed look, no matter how sharp his uniform really was.

"Will do." The dispatcher signed off. Duke finished off his burger and fries, and, sipping his super-sized cola, he put the cruiser in gear and moved slowly out into traffic heading south, toward Joseph and the lake.

CHAPTER 36

IT WAS EARLY MORNING, AND THE OLD HONDA CREPT UP INTO THE mountains to the west of Wallowa Lake, inching higher and higher, black smoke trailing out behind it. Big Cal was, of course, at the wheel. Jesse was beside him in the front passenger seat. And behind them were two others, both bound with duct tape and hunched over against each other. They were Viktor and Candi. For them it had been a long and terrifying night.

The previous evening Candi had been wandering down to the lakeshore when she saw Viktor being accosted by two men. From a distance she could barely make them out but they looked familiar. One was huge and wide. The other was tall with long black hair that hung down his back. Viktor was talking in a loud voice, as if he were unhappy to be with them and kept backing away from them. As she got closer she could see, to her surprise, it was Big Cal and Jesse. What the hell are they doing here, she thought, as she rushed toward them.

Jesse looked up to see Candi charging at them. He had a gun in his hand and was directing Viktor into the back of the Honda. He pushed Viktor the rest of the way in and turned his attention to Candi. This had not been part of the plan.

"What the fuck are you doin'?" Candi demanded. She had lost all her Christian charm and had reverted to her Titty bar vocabulary. She lunged at Jesse. Then she saw the gun in his hands and stopped dead in her tracks. "What the shit?"

"Stand back, Candi," Jesse demanded. "Just stand back. This

138

ain't your affair." "The hell it isn't. What do you two think you're doing?" She looked at Cal, who was trying, somehow, to hide his massive body behind the Honda."Cal?"

"We got business with this guy," Cal said. "Okay?"

"We're going to have to take her with us," Jesse said. He directed the gun at her again, and motioned her into the car. Candi looked around, hoping there would be someone who could help. The lakeshore was deserted and dark. There was no one.

Jesse pushed her into the back of the car next to Viktor. They looked at each other, too paralyzed with fear to speak. Cal got in behind the wheel and Jesse sat in the front passenger seat, leaning back over the seat to keep watch on their captives.

"Where are you taking us?" Candi demanded to know. "And what the hell are you two even doing up here?"

"Shut up," said Jesse. "You're fuckin' up the program as it is."

They were heading north, around the lake toward Joseph. Within minutes they pulled into the motel and parked at the far end of the parking lot, away from the overhead lighting. Jesse pushed them toward the door of their unit while Cal unlocked the door. Inside, they wrapped duct tape around Candi's arms and legs and put a piece over her mouth and pushed her onto the chair in the corner. They wrapped Viktor's arms and legs too, but left his mouth uncovered.

"We'll stay until morning and then we want to leave early and head to the mountains." Jesse spread a map out on the small table that served as a dining table. "The trailhead we want is about fifteen miles from here."

Big Cal nodded. This was not going as planned. He looked at Candi lying in the corner, her eyes wide and panicked. Why couldn't she just have minded her own business? Viktor was babbling in some foreign tongue as he sat at the end of one of the beds. Probably Russian, Cal thought. Gibberish.

"Shut the fuck up, old man," said Jesse. He emphasized his comment with a wave of the pistol. Viktor had dealt with enough homicidal maniacs in his life to know when to do just that. He went silent.

The night was long and no one got any sleep. Candi lay where she had been thrown. Viktor crouched in another corner. Jesse and Cal took turns keeping watch and each tried to get some sleep while the other was on duty. But they didn't get much. Jesse smoked some weed while he watched television infomercials.

At about 5 a.m., while it was still dark, Jesse rousted Cal and they packed their gear and quietly took it all out to the car. Then the prisoners were pulled to their feet; the duct was tape removed from their ankles, and they were marched to the car and pushed into the back seat. With the headlights off, they crept slowly out of the parking lot and headed toward the outskirts of town, where a McDonald's was just opening for the morning. Cal parked in a dark corner of the lot and Jesse went inside and ordered sausage and egg biscuits and coffee for the two of them. He bought nothing for Candi or Viktor. Then they headed out of town and toward the Wallowa Mountains, up toward the Eagle Cap Wilderness, just as dawn was beginning to spread itself across the landscape.

For a while they drove through cattle country, past herds grazing lazily in clusters, and then, gradually, the elevation gain began, taking them into forested areas where steep rock cliffs rose above them. The old Honda groaned with the climb and the extra weight it was carrying. It was used to Cal, gigantic as he was, and could even tolerate a passenger like Jesse. But the two in the back seat were more than it wished to accommodate. It crept up the highway, barely making it from wide turn to wide turn. Fortunately there was no other traffic at all. They had the road to themselves.

Jesse had taken Viktor's wallet from him the night before and was now thumbing through it, hoping it might contain some valuable information about his bank accounts. There were only a couple of credit cards, which Jesse immediately pocketed for himself, and a few dollars in cash. Not even a driver's license. No personal information at all, other than Viktor's permanent alien resident card.

"Shit, he ain't even a citizen," said Jesse to Cal, looking over at the beefy profile of his accomplice.

"Vat ish it you vant?" pleaded Viktor.

"Shut up," yelled Jesse, turning back and glaring at Viktor. "Just shut the fuck up."

Viktor lapsed back into silence. The car slowly ground on in low gear, struggling to make it up to the next turn in the road.

CHAPTER 37

Sheriff Jon Wain pulled into the campground, still wiping ketchup from the side of his mouth and sucking on his super-sized cola. Harvey had gotten there before him and was chatting with a group of people standing just outside the front entrance of the campground administration building. Wain pulled himself up to his full five foot five, took a swipe at the toes of his cowboy boots to make sure they had a bit of a shine, and approached his sergeant.

"What the hell's goin' on, Harvey?" He looked around at the circle of worried faces.

"Two folks are missin'," Harvey said. He had his notebook out and was writing down what folks had been telling him. "Some old Russian guy name of," he looked down at his notes, "Viktor Karshenko." He paused. "He is seventy-eight years old and one of the instructors of this conference. The star, from what they tell me." He consulted his notes once again. "The other person missing is a young woman, one of the students, name of Candice Summers, a college student from Oregon City. No one has seen either of them since last night at the evening prayer service here in the Great Hall. Ms. Summers, who goes by the name of "Candi" was last seen heading down to the lake. She told one of her roommates that she wanted to sit by the lake for a while. She never came back. Nobody saw where Karshenko went after the service. One guy said he thought he saw him leave early."

"Maybe they just took off together," mused Sheriff Jon. "May not be a kidnapping at all."

"Well, we don't know for sure, but the feelin' here is that they didn't have much in common and were not in any way involved with one another, if you know what I mean."

"Yeah, I know what you mean. Either she wasn't puttin' out for him, or he couldn't do much about it if she would." He chuckled.

At that point Nell came up to them. "She didn't come back to the yurt last night and we worried all night long. I reported it to Reverend Benson but he said we should wait until this morning to do anything." She paused. "He didn't seem too concerned with."

Redd Benson was, in fact, beside himself. Nothing like this had ever happened at God+Write before. This could screw up everything. There would be bad publicity. The TV stations would no doubt start going through their archives and come up with reruns of the pedophile episodes and they would be shown endlessly for the next few weeks, no matter what the outcome here. Joseph might be at the end of the world, but, shit, they did have TV. And with Karshenko gone, for whatever reason, there goes the hope of a handsome endowment. That would mean no salary increase for him next year, let alone some better office furniture.

"Has there been any communication from anyone regarding this matter?" asked Sheriff Wain, trying his best to sound official. Everyone shook their heads.

Harvey got descriptions of both Karshenko and Candi, and if what folks recalled they had been wearing when last seen. Redd Benson found a photo of Viktor taken from his personnel file and gave it to Harvey.

This was most strange, Harvey thought. An old man who could barely speak English and a young pretty woman who would not likely have been attracted to him. It didn't sound as though they would have taken off together voluntarily.

"This is Professor Russell Kees," said Harvey, introducing

Russell to Sheriff Wain. "He may have been the last person to see Ms. Summers."

Russell was clearly distraught. His relationship with Candi was just taking off. Of course, he did not share that with anyone else. "She and I were to meet after the prayer service so I could go over some poems she had written." He paused to emphasize the fact that he was performing some strictly professorial function and not hoping to get into her short-shorts. "She is both a student of mine at East Hills Liberty College in Oregon City, and here in my poetry workshop."

"And she didn't show up for your "get-together?" asked Sheriff Wain. He stared up directly into Russell's eyes. Russell felt himself tense. He suddenly thought of poor Lucy so far away.

"No. I waited for her but she didn't show up."

Sheriff Wain filed Russell's name in the back of his mind as, perhaps, a serious person of interest. He looked like a horny fucker and this might well have been a liaison that went bad. He might very well have tried to come on to her and she might have resisted.

Next they then interviewed both Redd and Pastor Bob Fairly. Neither claimed to have seen either Viktor or Candi after the services the night before. Redd seemed sincere in his denials. Pastor Bob, however, was sweating bullets, despite the fact that the morning temperature was still cool. He denied even knowing either of the missing people very well. Massive wet circles had broken through under the armpits of the heavy wool leisure suit he was wearing. Another possibility for further scrutiny, thought Sheriff Wain.

One by one they took the conferees, faculty members and staff to one side and questioned them closely. No new information was forthcoming. The grounds were thoroughly searched for any clues to the missing persons. There was nothing found that shed any light on their whereabouts. The mystery remained.

It was later that day when the first cell phone call was received by Redd Benson.

CHAPTER 38

IT WAS A LITTLE PAST MID-MORNING WHEN BIG CAL AND JESSE AND their "guests" arrived at the area of the trailhead that Jesse had chosen for their hike up into the Eagle Cap. Jesse had the map on his lap and was watching intently as they rounded the last curve and he could see the sign indicating the presence of trailheads.

"There, right over there." He pointed off to his right at a widening in the two- lane road. "I think that's the place. That must be it."

Big Cal pulled the creaking Honda off the pavement and they lurched and bumped their way to a barren patch of ground well out of sight of the road. He turned off the motor and the wheezing car coughed a couple of times, spit out some smoke, and fell silent, seemingly glad to be at rest. Cal looked back at Viktor and Candi, both still bound by the duct tape, with more over their mouths. Candi's eyes were watching everything Cal and Jesse did. Viktor, on the other hand, was just sitting back, hunched over, his eyes closed.

"Okay," said Jesse, getting out of the car. "We need to get the gear out of the back and get ready to head out." He liked that kind of talk: "gear" and "head out." He thought it made him sound like he knew what he was doing up here. His Indian blood was surging. It was too bad Candi had stuck her nose into the situation when she did; but that was just the way it was. Maybe at some point she'd see that she might benefit from what they were doing and go along with it. Maybe a quarter of a million dollars would spark her interest. Until then, she'd best be kept taped up like Viktor.

Jesse loaded up Cal like a pack mule, huge knapsack on his

back, more stuff loaded on top of that, more equipment hanging around his neck and his waist. Jesse pulled his own backpack up onto his back too, and loaded up old Viktor as well, after he had undone the tape on his arms and legs. At this point Viktor was without resistance. He was going with the flow. He had no idea who these people were or why they were doing this to him. He went where they told him to go, pushing him toward the entrance to the trail. They had removed the tape from Candi's arms and legs too, and then removed the tape from her mouth. Jesse figured that there wasn't anywhere she could go now. There was no one else around for God knows how far. They hadn't seen another car in an hour.

But she had plenty to say. "Jesse, you mother fucker, what the hell do you think you're doin'?"

Jesse tried to calm her down. "Look, I know you're pissed, but you gotta realize, you stuck your nose in where it didn't belong." He pushed her onto the trail and they began hiking. Viktor was being led up the forested incline; Cal trudging on behind like a pack mule. "We got a plan we're workin' out," Jesse continued. " You damn near fucked it up. So keep quiet now and do what you're told. We got a ways to go."

"What kind of plan, you asshole? Can't you see he's an old, old man? You're goin' to kill him if you're not careful."

Jesse looked at Candi and smiled his best Nez Perce smile. "Yeah. He's a *RICH* old man."

"What do you mean, rich? And what difference does that make for you, even if it's true?"

"He's worth over a million dollars. He won some prize that put that kinda dough in his pocket." Jesse paused, as he was getting a bit winded himself. "We're goin' to get some of it outta his pocket." He looked at Viktor. "Maybe half of it, for starters. Maybe all of it, if he don't play along."

Viktor turned to look at him. He had no idea what he was

talking about. Candi could barely contain herself. "And just how do you think you're going to end up with his money?"

"If he wants to get out of here alive, we will," Jesse said. "We're going to keep him here until he gets us into his Swiss bank accounts, or wherever. Once we have that information, then we arrange for him to transfer the money and we get out of the country. Belize is on our list. You can come along and enjoy the good life with me, or not."

Candi shook her head. "You're both crazy as loons," she said.

They hiked for another hour, resting from time to time. Cal was not in the best shape, and given the fact that he was carrying the biggest load, had to stop and drink from his new canteen frequently. Once he went into the bushes to pee. Jesse figured they had about five more miles to go, climbing all through rugged terrain. The air was getting thinner and the sun was beginning its early descent. Jesse had researched the trails into the Eagle Cap and this was one of the least used in summer. It should eventually lead to the stone hut he had read about that was used in the winter by skiers. He was certain that they could stay there until the mission was a success. So far they had encountered no one either coming down or coming up behind them. Nor had there been any sign of helicopters overhead. Just blue sky with a few wispy clouds. Every now and then they would hear some movement in the dense forest, some crashing about, which spooked Cal no end. But they saw nothing. The occasional scat of deer or elk on the trail. Once in a while they would come to a mountain stream coming down, twisting and turning toward lower ground and eventually the river. Candi had no alternative but to go along with the program at this point. She would bide her time, she decided. She would never have imagined that Jesse had the balls to try something like this. And that he had roped big dumb Cal in was the topper.

Viktor struggled to keep up. His new Walmart hiking boots were again raising blisters on his poor feet, and the pack they had put on his back was sliding back and forth, causing his shoulders and back to hurt. His knees hurt. His hips hurt. His head hurt. He was short of breath. Jesse kept pushing at him whenever he slowed down. "Move it along, old man," he would mutter. "Move it along."

The sun had dropped behind the line of mountains to the west when they finally reached their destination. Indeed, there was the small stone hut, forlorn and deserted. It was open, with no window glass, no door. Inside there were no amenities whatsoever. It was shelter and nothing more. There was a small stone fireplace and some dry firewood, however, and they could keep warm at night with that.

"Welcome home," said Jesse, as he dropped his pack on the ground. "Welcome home."

CHAPTER 39

Sheriff Wain was on the radio with his dispatcher. Thus far they didn't have a clue about what could have happened to the missing conferees. The occupant of one of the private cabins, a middle-aged man who had been sitting out on his porch at the time, reported having seen an older car, perhaps a Japanese make, but not sure, near the campground last night late. He hadn't seen who was in it, but he thought he'd heard some yelling, like it might have been a girl or a woman. When he went out into his yard to look, the car pulled away and that was the end of it. He recalled that the car was old and was burning a lot of oil, smoking badly. It might have been gray or dirty white.

"We'd better start thinking about a search and rescue effort," Wain said. "At least we need to be ready. If those two were snatched by kidnappers, there aren't many places they could take them and hold them. They could be taking them up into the wilderness area. That might just be their plan. We'd best be prepared." He paused to check the shine on his boots. "And alert the state police to be on the lookout for the car, as well as the local folks in every town between here and La Grande."

The dispatcher agreed and said he would begin getting their volunteers together and have them meet Wain at the campground first thing in the morning.

So far the only lead was the sighting of the older car late last night near the campground. The workshops for the day had been cancelled and everywhere conferees were just wandering aimlessly.

There was some fear that they also might be in danger of being assaulted or abducted. The women were especially fearful and were staying grouped together. By late in the day Sheriff Wain had decided to bring in the Oregon State Police, and several officers came over from La Grande and became part of the base team. About that time a report came in that two men had left the Indian Chief Motel without paying their bill. They had left early in the morning without checking out. They had been there the better part of a week and had used a stolen credit card. They had been driving an older Honda automobile, gray in color, and it had an Oregon license number from a stolen plate. One man had registered as Jimmie Eagle Feather. The other, a huge man was known to one of the room maids as Cal.

Sheriff Wain took the information and added it to what he had accumulated already in his investigation. It might mean nothing at all. But then, he had nothing at all to go on at this point. Then the first call came in. it was a cell phone call to Redd Benson, who was sitting in his office pondering the downfall of his plans for the future.

"Benson," he snapped into the phone on his desk.

"Listen, and listen good." A raspy voice on the other end came in over considerable static. "I will say this only once. We have the old guy. We will release him when we have received access to his bank accounts and have successfully withdrawn $500,000.00 and it has been transferred to an offshore account we designate. At such time as he has agreed to cooperate with us, he will be in touch with you and will instruct you what to do next. If you do not follow those instructions to the letter, he will not be on this earth for long." The voice paused. "Do not attempt to locate us or call the police or the old fart will surely never be returned alive." No mention was made of Candi. The phone went dead.

Redd sat for a few moments with the receiver in his hand. Shit, he thought. Why did we bring that old bastard out here anyway. We can't understand a word he says and he brings this shitpile down on us. He then called in Sheriff Wain to share this development. It had now been confirmed. There had been a kidnapping. The state police investigators were brought up to speed on this development too. Harvey had sent Carl, one of his deputies over to the Indian Chief Motel to interview the desk clerk and the other employees and peruse the registration documents and comb through the room they had occupied for clues and fingerprints.

More reports began coming in of purchases made of a pistol at the gun show over in Enterprise with a stolen credit card and purchases of camping gear made at Walmart with the same stolen card. Sheriff Wain decided he would interview the gun dealer and the Walmart employees himself. A pattern was beginning to emerge and they were starting to get some leads that might actually take them somewhere.

Wain swung his cruiser out of the parking lot of the campground and headed north around the lake, passing through Joseph. It was dinnertime and the town had quieted down, its broad streets almost empty of either parked cars or moving traffic. A few cars were parked near the tavern on Main Street and as he passed the Indian Chief Motel he could see his deputy's cruiser still parked in front of the registration office. He continued north on Highway 82 to Enterprise and stopped first at the Walmart to interview the employees there. He was ushered into a back office where the manager and two employees sat waiting for him. They described in detail as best they could the two men, one huge and other an Italian-looking guy, with long, black hair, who had bought all kinds of outdoor equipment earlier. No one had seen what type of car they were driving. After they had gone it was determined that the credit card used had been reported stolen a short time before. The amount owing was in excess of $400.00. Wain thanked them for their help and headed on to the local second hand store where the gun show was always held. They were just closing when he arrived. He located the man who had sold the gun. He was reluctant to talk too freely with the Sheriff as there were some serious questions as to whether or not the law had been broken in the course of the transaction. Still the man was out almost $300.00 for the pistol and the ammo. And ammo was scarce and hard to come by these days. He was pissed, to say the least. His anger overcame his reluctance to report the crime.

Sheriff Wain soon found himself back at Dinty's Burgers once again enjoying the Doublepounder Valu-Meal. This time he sat inside at one of the little anchored tables and mused over what had happened and what leads - if any - were developing. Soon his deputy, Carl, joined him and brought him up to speed on his interview of the motel clerk and their finds in the room the two men had occupied. It had been a long day and the two police officers just sat staring through the large window of the fast food joint, watching the traffic drift by, eating their Valu-Meals and slurping their colas. Carl already had a smear of catsup down the front of his tie. Sheriff Wain looked at him with some measure of disgust on his face. After all, ever the" Duke," he was neat as a pin.

CHAPTER 40

JESSE HAD TAPED CANDI'S WRISTS AND ANKLES TOGETHER AGAIN TO make sure she didn't try to take off. He and Cal had put up the tent next to the little stone hut and put her and Viktor into it, laying them down on the cold ground cloth. It was now dark and the forest seemed to be overtaking their campsite. Cal had built a fire in the little fireplace inside the hut and he and Jesse were huddled around it. They had cooked some of the freeze-dried dinners they had bought at the Walmart store for dinner and were now taking swigs from the bottle of cheap local scotch, and Jesse was smoking a joint.

"What are we going to do with Candi," asked Cal? Her kidnapping had not been part of the plan. He was beginning to have very mixed feelings about this whole project.

"She'll just have to stay with us. We can't take a chance of her runnin' off and finding her way out of here." Jesse sucked deep on the roach and held the smoke for as long as he could, then exhaled. "Besides, once she sees all that money, she'll come around."

Cal shook his head. Somewhere, deep in the dark forest that surrounded them, an owl let out a hooting sound. Farther up the mountainside they could hear the crashing of some animal, some creature that sounded as though it might be a pretty good size. Cal had never spent a night in the wilderness before. This was not his idea of a good time. But Jesse was hyped. His Indian heritage was coming to the fore.

"This is how it was in the old days," said Jesse, as if he had any idea what it might have been like in the old days. "We lived off the land, moving from place to place. Never resting in any one spot." He took his new hunting knife from its sheath and examined the blade, testing it for sharpness. He took the bottle from Cal and took another drink of scotch. From the interior of the tent they could hear Candi's complaints.

"Shut the fuck up," yelled Jesse, turning in disgust. "There ain't no one around, so it won't do you no good to try and bug us."

Vikktor had fallen asleep, turned onto his side, his body twisted in an awkward fashion. How he could sleep like that Candi had no idea. His hands and feet were taped like hers, but he was offering no resistance at all. His breathing was labored. Soon both Cal and Jesse came into the tent to check on them. There were no sleeping bags for either Candi or Viktor. Cal gave Candi his parka to give her some warmth. She actually smiled at him. After all, this was the man who had protected her at the club. What had happened to that? How could he have gotten mixed up with Jesse?

Soon, as a full moon rose above the trees, with Jesse and Cal stretched out on the floor of the hut in their new sleeping bags. All four of them fell into a troubled sleep. Candi was contemplating her fate and what she'd do to Jesse if she ever got the chance. Viktor was wondering what the hell was going on. Cal was already dreaming of the Larry Singer Show, with Candi at his side, cheering and jumping up and down. And Jesse was off to Belize, getting it on with some chick and counting his money. Huge piles of money.

CHAPTER 41

RUSSELL HAD NOT SLEPT SINCE CANDI HAD DISAPPEARED. IN HIS OWN way, he felt some sense of responsibility. After all, she had been on her way to meet with him and he'd had hopes that they might even take their new relationship to a new level. Thoughts of *The Power of the Moment* had been surging in him. He had almost heard Zuber murmering in his ear that this might, indeed, be just the moment. But then she didn't appear. At first he thought perhaps Candi might have decided against it. But then he learned the truth and was both distressed and relieved at the same time. The entire conference was now on hold. Nothing was happening. There were no workshops, no readings. Only the frequent prayer gatherings to seek God's help in finding and returning both Viktor and Candi safely and soon. So far the prayers weren't working. The police were everywhere. A volunteer search and rescue club had arrived and its members were preparing to hike up into the Eagle Cap Wilderness in the morning, seeking clues to the missing comrades. Given the purchases that the suspected kidnappers had made of a gun and outdoor equipment, it was assumed they must be somewhere in the wilderness area. But the wilderness area was huge and rugged. Helicopters had been ordered from the army base outside of Pendleton but overcast skies were hampering the effort to spot the kidnappers and their hostages. Russell planned to join the searchers. He did not feel he could just sit by and not do something, even if he didn't really know what he was doing.

Pastor Bob Fairly was also disconcerted by the events of the week. He was leading the prayer gatherings and his repertoire of prayers was running low. He was usually good for a Sunday morning service, a Sunday evening service, and a Wednesday evening service. But this every day emergency sort of thing requiring daily public prayer was beyond his storehouse of godly connections. Even his resonant baritone voice was starting to give out. But he was doing his best.

The conferees hung around the Great Hall throughout the day, awaiting any word about the abduction. News of the mysterious cell phone call had been kept from the general camp population so that it could be fully analyzed without distraction. Only the police and Redd Benson knew about it. They were, even now, trying to trace it. So far with no success. The only thing they knew for certain was that the caller was within cell-phone range, but barely.

Russell returned to the cabin he had been sharing with Viktor and climbed into bed. Oddly enough, he felt he was going to miss the snoring and wheezing that had accompanied his rest the past week. The silence of the cabin and the surrounding forest was deafening. He thought of Lucy away in Mt. Vernon. And then his thoughts turned once again to Candi. He could smell the magic odor of her shampoo. With the scent of her drifting through his thoughts, he finally fell back into a fitful sleep. He dreamed of what the power of the moment might have had in store for him.

CHAPTER 42

THE FOLLOWING MORNING THE SEARCH AND RESCUE TEAMS WERE organized and ready to head off in search of Candi and Viktor. The volunteers knew the Eagle Cap Wilderness from years of hiking the trails and backpacking into the interior to the upper lakes and in all kinds of weather. They broke off into individual teams and plotted out which team would go where. There was an immense area to cover. In the meantime, police cars were driving the backroads leading to the various trailheads in an attempt to locate the car that had been used in the abduction, and helicopters were again flying in from Pendleton to take part in the search. The sky had cleared so that there was hope they might spot something or someone. So far, however, nothing had been discovered.

Russell asked to join with one of the search parties. He strapped on his hiking boots and packed his backpack with water, some energy bars and a few other items he thought he might need. While he was not one to normally go hiking, and especially over such rugged terrain, he felt he needed to go. He harbored some notion that he might actually find and rescue poor Candi. Toward noon, the rescue teams, connected to one another by radio, waited for the word to come to begin their arduous trek up into the Eagle Cap wilderness.

Meanwhile, Sheriff Wain and his deputies had put together a profile of Jesse and Cal. They had a mug shot of Jesse from a prior arrest and a police artist had done a drawing of Cal from discriptions of witnesses. The word was out for the searchers to keep an eye out for the old Honda, which was registered to Cal, and any sign of their whereabouts. While they were operating on the assumption that the kidnappers had gone into the Eagle Cap still they could not be sure of that at this time. They needed to be alert to other possibilities. Police in every local jurisdiction were on alert. All points bulletins had been sent out. Redd Benson was told to stay near the phone in the event another call should come in and arrangements had been made to record and try to trace such calls.

Pastor Bob thought about joining a search team but finally decided not to. He really was not equipped for such an outdoor, woodsy experience. He did not have a leisure suit that he felt would really be appropriate for a climb up those mountains He was certain that his tasseled loafers would not survive the trek. He had not counted on any of this when he signed on at God+Write. While he didn't mind humping Candi whenever he might get the opportunity, he didn't feel it was his God-given duty to go looking for her. And certainly not for Viktor, who had not yet offered any endowments that would have made Pastor Bob's life so much easier. In fact there was a good likelihood that this adventure would lead to Viktor losing a good deal of his purported wealth and what good would he be to Pastor Bob then? Others of able body attending the conference also joined the search teams and all of the scheduled activities for the conference were cancelled. Those who were not able to participate in the search effort stayed behind and prayed. Pastor Bob's time was taken up by thinking of new and exciting things to talk about with the Lord.

It wasn't easy.

CHAPTER 43

JESSE WOKE TO THE SUN SHINING THROUGH THE OPEN WINDOW OF THE stone hut. Even in his new down sleeping bag he was cold. He looked over at Cal, a huge lump wrapped in his mummy bag that he wore like a giant sausage skin. He was still asleep and his breathing moved the bag up and down. Jesse was beginning to rethink his Indian heritage. He had assumed that somehow he would instinctively know what needed to be done and how to do it out here in the wild. But he had to admit, at least to himself, that he did not. He had had a hell of a time making the fire last night. He had matches and everything he should have needed. But still, it took forever to flame up. They had run out of dry firewood, and he hadn't counted on the new wood being green or wet. He couldn't think what his ancestors would have done. Even Candi had laughed at him.

He pulled himself out of his sleeping bag and smoothed back his tangle of curly hair. He moved over to the small camp stove that Cal had hauled up along with most of the rest of the gear, lit it and put a small pot of water on to boil. They had brought some instant coffee with them. As he was doing this Candi called out from the tent. Jesse looked in to see what she wanted.

"Undo me, you asshole." She complained. "I need to take a pee, bad, and I don't want to do it right here."

Jesse untaped her wrists and ankles and watched as she went off into the woods. A short time later she returned just as Jesse was pouring a cup of the coffee for himself. He held the pot up for her and she took it and poured a cup for herself. As she drank she watched him closely. What the hell was he thinking, she wondered. She shook her head in disgust and looked around. Here she was to hell and gone. She had no clothes other than what she was wearing. No nothing.

Cal was starting to move around. Candi could hear his farts rumbling from across the campsite. Soon he came out of the hut and looked at her and Jesse. He smiled weakly at Candi. Jesse glared at him. A short time later Jesse passed out an energy bar to each of them. Cal looked at his as though Jesse had laid a turd in his hand. Candi took the wrapper off hers and nibbled at it. Viktor was still in the tent, apparently sleeping. Jesse decided not to disturb the old bastard.

By mid-morning Jesse had decided that it might be time to make another phone call and to get his plan rolling. He needed to get the necessary information from Viktor so that they could access his bank accounts and arrange the transfer of funds. He yelled to Viktor to get up and then went into the tent to talk to him. He didn't know how cooperative Viktor would be. Thus far he had denied having any wealth. Viktor was still lying where he had been the night before when Jesse checked on him. He shook Viktor's shoulder and spoke in his ear. "Time to wake up, old man. Time to hit the trail." There was no response. He shook him again. There was still no response. Shit, thought Jesse. What's goin' on here. He shook him harder. Viktor did not move. Jesse felt his forehead. It was ice cold.

"Oh Shit! Holy Christ!"

Candi heard Jesse yelling and Cal came bursting out of the hut. They dashed into the tent to see Jesse bent over Viktor.

"The old bastard's fuckin' gone," said Jesse, pointing down at the lifeless body on the ground. "He's fuckin' gone."

"What do you mean, gone?" asked Candi, looking down at Viktor.

"He's right there," said Cal, pointing at the ground.

Candi knelt down and felt Viktor's wrist for any sign of a pulse. There was none. She turned up his face and it was a bluish gray color. He was already becoming stiff. "Christ Almighty, you've killed him," she yelled at Jesse and Cal. At that point panic set in. They had not anticipated this turn of events. Suddenly this entire venture was turning to shit. First Candi had gotten involved when she wasn't supposed to, and now Karshenko had turned up his toes.

Cal left the tent and sat on the ground like a giant boulder, not moving and with no expression on his big, dumb face. Candi had begun to cry. Jesse tried to think. It wasn't working. Here they were in the middle of nowhere with few provisions, a God-damned tent, and now, a stiff who was no longer worth a million bucks. No longer worth jack shit. Jesse shook Viktor one last time just to be sure. Viktor was most decidedly dead.

Suddenly they heard the sound of a helicopter passing over, far to the north of them. The sky was clear and blue this morning and they could see the helicopter silhouetted against the sun that had risen high above the outline of the mountains. It seemed to be headed their way.

"They must have figured out where we might be. Or else they're guessing," said Jesse. "Stay back, under the trees." He pushed Candi toward the tent, and Big Cal lumbered after them. They had erected the tent under a canopy of firs and Jesse did not think they would easily be seen from the air. This was the one thing he had probably planned that was accurate. They stayed still until it had passed over. There was no indication that they had been spotted.

"What do we do now?" asked Cal, as the drone of the copter's rotors became fainter and fainter in the clear mountain air.

"Yeah, smart ass. What are you going to do now?" Candi sneered at him. "Tell us what a real Nez Perce Indian would do now. "

Jesse thought for a little while. Then he motioned to Cal. "We are still going to make this work. We might not get a quarter million out of it, but we can get something. Enough to make it all worthwhile. They don't know he's dead. Where's your cell phone?"

Cal handed it to him and Jesse dialed the God + Write Conference administration office. Redd Benson, who had been waiting for such a call, answered. Jesse re-assumed his raspy voice. Redd motioned to the police officer who was sitting at his side waiting to record and hopefully trace just such a call.

"Listen jerk, I am not going to repeat myself.' Jesse said. " Karshenko is here with us. We will call again tomorrow morning and you are to then have $100,000 in unmarked one hundred dollar bills in a suitcase and have a helicopter available. We will let you know when and where. Again, if you notify the law or don't follow these instructions to the letter, Karshenko will die." With that he hit the end button. He turned the phone off to preserve the battery and handed it back to Cal.

Jesse was beginning to conclude this adventure into his Indian heritage was not what he had hoped it would be.

CHAPTER 44

S HERIFF WAIN WAS IMMEDIATELY NOTIFIED THAT THE KIDNAPPERS HAD made contact again. He was having coffee at the Coffee Grind and talking to Tillie, the barista, when his radio crackled. He quickly responded and headed back to the conference grounds. There he met with his deputies and communicated with the leaders of the search and rescue teams by radio. The call had been faint and riddled with static, barely audible.

"They're almost out of reception range," said Wain. "That would suggest that they're somewhere up in the wilderness area, for sure."

"We've been up all the roads into the Eagle Cap," said Harvey. "So far, nothing."Harvey paused to look at his map again.

"There's a group of trailheads here," Wain said, pointing on the map to a location several more miles up. "I think we should send a car up there and have one of the copters do a fly over and see if they can either spot a group of people or at least a car."

Harvey nodded and immediately dispatched one of the deputies to the area.

"Why the hell those crazy bastards would go up there is beyond me," said Wain, shaking his head in wonder.

"According to the desk clerk at the motel they stiffed, one of the two men, who claimed to be named Jimmy Eage Feather, also claimed to be Nez Perce, although the clerk said he didn't look like it. He thought the guy looked more Italian than Indian, but who ever knows these days? Anyway, he was struttin' his stuff and bragging about his Indian heritage and how they had at one time owned all this territory, and how the white man had stolen it. And of course, we know they bought a bunch of camping gear. Why else would they do that?" Harvey scratched his oversized nose and pulled his sagging pants up over his oversized gut. Sheriff Wain was, as usual, immaculately dressed, his uniform sharp and fresh.

"Well, we know something has gone wrong, wherever they are, since now they are asking for a specific amount of money rather than bank account information." Sheriff Wain paused. "Something has happened and it sounds like they are getting a little desperate."

The search teams had been waiting for some break in the case to give them an idea of where to begin the search. There were about thirty men, all dressed in mountaineering clothing. They carried backpacks loaded with enough provisions to last them a week in the wild if necessary. They were all experienced, as every summer, and sometimes in the winter, climbers and hikers or skiers would get into trouble in the Eagle Cap when they got lost or injured, or worse, and these men were the ones who went up after them. They came from all around. Some were ranchers, farmers, storeowners, school teachers and even a local artist or two. All were drawn to the cause by their love of the wilderness and their desire to be part of what maintaining wilderness meant. Now they stood around, drinking coffee and talking. They were impatient to get started.

The conferees, on the other hand, were far less disciplined in their response to what had happened. They milled around, aimlessly, despite the frequent prayer meetings and talk of God's will and what a lovely girl Candi was. They told each other how strange that a man so highly regarded as Viktor Karshenko, after all he had faced in his life, should now be forced to deal with a challenge such as this. Nell and Russell found themselves talking often about Candi, each from his or her own perspective. But both had seen Candi as more than just a friend. Each had brought a certain hope to the relationship that had not yet fully matured. Russell wanted to take her to bed. The truth was, however, Nell did too. This was information that they did not share with each other.

By mid-afternoon a call came in from the deputy who had gone to check out the area of trailheads that Wain had suggested. An old Honda had been found. The vehicle number matched the information the police had on Cal. The car was parked off the roadway, somewhat hidden from view by a thick grove of fir trees. It could not have been seen from the air and since it was primer gray the vehicle could barely be seen, even from the road. But there it was, abandoned.

There were a series of trails, at least a half dozen, that left from that location. Which trail the suspects might have taken was still an unknown. Sheriff Wain immediately took off from the camp-ground and headed back around the lake, then south, up into the wilderness area to the trailheads. The other deputies followed, as did the leaders of the search teams. It was time to spring into action. They had a genuine lead at last.

The Honda was thoroughly examined for any clues indicating where the occupants might have gone. There was little to go on. Cal had not bothered to lock it, since there was nothing in it to steal and he didn't figure that anyone would want to steal the car itself. The police and searchers found little other than some torn pieces of gray duct tape, cigarette butts, residue of marijuana, empty bottles, and candy bar wrappers.

"I would suggest we send a team up each trail, keeping in radio contact, and see where it leads." Wain had spread a map out on the hood of the Honda and was pointing out the different trails. "We need to be extremely careful as we know these guys are going to be increasingly dangerous as we close in on them. And remember, they have at least one weapon. They may be nuts, but that's what also makes them dangerous. As well as desperate."

The others nodded. The excitement of the search was now taking hold. This was what they lived for: not only the challenge of the wilderness, but the possibility of saving a young woman and an old man from harm, and bringing criminals to justice. They broke off into groups of about six searchers each and Wain noted which team was going to head onto which trail. He had also been in touch with the helicopters and one was now coming over from the little municipal airport at Enterprise to do a fly-over and report. He could already hear its engines whining in the distance. With that he gave the orders to head out.

CHAPTER 45

JESSE WAS GETTING MORE AND MORE AGITATED. HIS FACE WAS TWITCHING as if he had stuck his dick in a light socket. Karshenko had met the Big Ruski in the sky during the night, and Candi was giving him shit constantly. Big Cal, dumb as a brick, was sitting there motionless like the mountain itself, silent and blank, an ugly scowl on his ugly face. The last call to the conference grounds had not left Jesse feeling like the plan was really coming together. In fact, the plan seemed to have turned to shit on him. He sat playing with the pistol, aiming it at this and that. The day had warmed up, but there was still a chill in the air. He was still cold from last night. It had been cold enough to freeze your nuts off, he thought, as he chewed listlessly on an energy bar. He didn't feel very much energy coursing through his Nez Perce veins. He was certain his ancestors had never had to eat this crap. Overhead he could hear the drone of another helicopter approaching the mountainside. They had been flying over almost every hour or two, sometimes coming in low and sweeping the area. Jesse had ordered Candi and Cal under the cover of the trees, and the tent was well hidden in the foliage. He was certain they could not be seen from the air. But still he realized that the police must have decided they were up here in the wilderness area and not somewhere in the valley. Somehow they must have traced his and Cal's actions of the last few days and were now on to them. Perhaps the cops had located the car. If so, it would just be a matter of time before they started sending searchers up the mountain. He and Cal would have to move, have to take Candi higher up into the Eagle Cap. Soon they would be out of cell phone range. The battery was almost gone now, anyway. But once they lost their only means of communication there would be no way they could arrange the transfer of the funds and plan their escape with the money. Crap, he thought, Nez Perce Indians get fucked again. History was repeating itself.

Jesse threw the energy bar wrapper into the coals of the fire he had built last night, and watched as it curled up into flame from the dying embers that were still smoking slightly. He'd better snuff that fire completely, he thought. He took a stick and scattered the ashes and watched as they slowly turned to white and gray and died away.

"Cal, get your ass over here and be useful for a change." Cal rose slowly and ambled over at Jesse's command.

"What you want, shit for brains?" Cal had finally figured out that they were in deep guano. He had spent a night lying on the cold ground, wrapped only in a sleeping bag, something he had never done before. He'd had nothing to eat but another fuckin' energy bar. If he ever saw another one of those in his lifetime it would be one too many. And then there was Candi. God Almighty, why did she have to be pulled into this? Even Cal could see that all was not right in wonderland.

"We need to close up camp here and head farther up the mountain. According to the map, there's a small lake, maybe fourteen miles or so more. If we can get there we can set up a better camp." Jesse pointed to a spot on the map. "There will be search parties comin' up here pretty soon." He casually aimed the pistol toward Cal, who jumped away.

"Watch where you're pointin' that thing," Cal said. His mood was getting darker and darker. Cal was not enthused about another fourteen miles of hiking up this rugged terrain. "What about Candi? What about the old fart? I ain't lungin' some dead guy on my back."

"Candi is fit. She's a dancer, for Chris' sake. She can handle it.

Probably better than you. We'll have to leave the old stiff here. He ain't goin' to care one way or the other. We'll cover him up in the brush." Jesse stuck the pistol in his belt and lit a cigarette, one of the last he had.

"You'll cover him up in the brush," sneered Cal. "I ain't touchin' no dead guy."

"Christ, you're a fuckin' pussy." Jesse said. "I don't know why I got tied up with you." He was already packing his backpack. Cal started to do the same. Candi was sulking off to one side. No one wanted to go into the tent and be with Viktor. But Viktor didn't seem to mind. He might as well have been back in Siberia.

CHAPTER 46

Sheriff Wain had called in the search dogs too, a pack of bloodhounds with extremely sensitive noses. They clustered around the old Honda, sniffing and sniffing. Wain had brought an item of Candi's clothing. Finally it seemed they may have picked up a trail. They headed toward one of the trailheads, a team of searchers following after, Sheriff Wain in the lead. Other searchers headed up other trails just to be sure they hadn't missed any opportunities to find the kidnappers and their hostages.

It was rugged going. The trail selected by the bloodhounds was rarely used and was not well maintained. The elevation gain was considerable, and the air was getting thinner and thinner. But for poor Harvey, who was having difficulty keeping up, the team made steady progress. Overhead they could see a helicopter circling around and around. They were in communication with it by radio but nothing had yet been spotted.

Periodically the searchers stopped to take a breather and have a drink of water. They had forded a couple of ice-cold streams and continued their ascent slowly but surely. Wain hadn't worked this hard in a long time, he thought. This was a hell of a lot more exciting than nabbing shoplifters at the local Safeway store or stopping some dude speeding through Lostine.

The dogs were loving the trek, branching out along the trail, sniffing and sniffing, working the ground with zeal. Their handlers were not enjoying it quite as much. It was tough going. But so far the weather was cooperating. While the temperatures dropped at night in the Wallowas, days were georgeous and clear at this time of year. Today the sky was blue, and there was a slight breeze. The temperature was warming. The search team could not have asked for a better day. Sound seemed to travel for miles. Now and then they would stop just to listen. So far, however, they had heard nothing that would give them any indication they were closing in on the kidnappers and the hostages.

By late afternoon the sun was dropping behind the line of the mountains and it was getting noticeably colder. At last the searchers came upon the stone hut which appeared to have been recently used. There were coals in the little fireplace that were still slightly warm. They could see where a tent had been set up, a grassy area trampled down, and the little stone hut, normally used in the winter by skiers, had clearly been occupied. They could see outlines in the dirt floor that showed where sleeping bags had been laid out on the ground. They found the torn wrappers of energy bars scattered here and there. Footprints were visible in the trampled grass.

"Let's look around some more before we head on," said Sheriff Wain, as some of the dogs lay down to take a rest and the men spread out to do a more thorough search of the surrounding area. It was not long before one of the men, with a dog straining on its leash, let out a yell.

"Over here, Sheriff."

Wain ran over to join him. The searcher was pointing to the ground under a large mountain laurel bush. He had swept back some of the brush to reveal a body. The bloodhound was nosing around it. Wain looked down at the remains of Viktor Karshenko. The old man was lying on his back, his blank eyes staring at the blue sky, his face stiff and knotted in death. He was still wearing his new hiking boots, made in El Salvador, and his new backpack, made in Tibet, was on the ground beside him. They could see marks in the ground that showed where his body had been dragged to the site.

"We're too late for this one," Wain said. "This has to be

Karshenko." The searchers gathered around, absorbing this defeat. At least they knew now that they were on the right trail. They only hoped they would be in time to save the young woman. They did a more thorough search, using the dogs, to determine whether there were any other bodies hidden anywhere. They found nothing more.

Wain left Viktor's body in the hands of the Scientific Investigation Unit, which had been brought in by helicopter when he had radioed their discovery. They immediately began scouring the area for further clues and information. A medical examiner had also been brought in and he immediately began examining Viktor's body to attempt to determine a cause of death. "We will eventually have to take the body to the county morgue in Enterprise for further examination and an autopsy," the examiner explained. "I don't find anything unusual here," he added. "No sign of trauma." He paused. "Maybe hypothermia. Maybe just a plain old heart attack."

Sheriff Wain nodded. It was time to move out and leave the investigators to their work. There were still two kidnappers at large out there and a young woman. The rest of the searchers moved on up the mountain as the helicopter lifted off from the open space where it had landed. Viktor was now safely laid out inside. He was now as stiff as those new hiking boots. The ones made in El Salvador.

CHAPTER 47

RUSSELL KEES HAD NOT BEEN ABLE OR WILLING TO JUST SIT BY AT THE conference center. When word had arrived of the discovery of Viktor's body, he hitched a ride to the site with the helicopter and had now joined the search party too. With the discovery of Viktor's body, he became even more agitated than he had been. While he was not equipped either with the necessary gear for wilderness survival or his own physical attributes, he trudged on ahead with Sheriff Wain and the rest of the search party. His shoes were inadequate and his legs were aching from the rugged climb. Still thoughts of Candi possibly needing him spurred him on. Sheriff Wain was not too pleased to have Kees along. He saw him as a drag on the effort, a tenderfoot, as they now had to maintain a slower pace up the side of the mountain to allow Russell to keep pace with them. He viewed time as of the essence, having discovered the dead Russian already. Who knows what more desperate crimes might be commited now that the search team might actually be closing in on the killers? Clearly the entire scheme had disintegrated and was ending badly for the kidnappers. Desperate, they might do anything to Candi Summers, who was now, it clearly appeared, a hostage.

Slowly the rescue party moved steadily up the steep terrain. It was getting late and night was falling quickly. The searchers did not have much more time. They could not risk injury to the climbers by trying to continue after dark. They needed to find a spot where they could set up camp and spend the night. Soon they came to a clearing and Sheriff Wain announced that they would stay the night here. Only Russell was not pleased with this news. Despite his exhaustion, and aching legs and back, he wanted to press on. He sensed that the power of the moment was at hand. In his mind Zuber's voice kept spurring him on. That and traces of Candi's perfume that lingered in his memory. And so although Wain asked him not to, he continued on up the trail.

"Whatever you do, don't fuck this up," warned Wain. "Don't try to be a hero. Those bastards have at least one weapon that we know of. They might have more." He paused. "In any event, one is enough to God-damn well kill you."

But Russell stumbled off into the darkness. Sheriff Wain and the other members of the search party settled in for the night. Little did they realize then that they would never see Russell Kees, MFA, again.

CHAPTER 48

Back at the conference center Redd Benson and Pastor Bob Fairly were doing their best to keep a lid on the debacle. They didn't want to spook the other conferees or, worse yet, the God+Write sponsors, patrons and financial supporters. If word got out that one of their faculty members had been kidnapped, along with one of the students, all hell would break loose. Redd stayed by the phone, waiting to see if another call might come in from the kidnappers. A reserve deputy was with him to try to trace the call and record it. Pastor Bob was off to one side of the Great Hall, busy praying up a storm. His leisure suit was now less than neatly pressed, his usually shiny, tasseled loafers now muddy and unkempt. So far the Good Lord had not checked in with His faithful servants. All in all, He seemed to be taking a hands-off approach to the whole affair.

"Dear Lord, Keeper of the universe," prayed Pastor Bob, down on his knees. "Don't let the money dry up." From the other side of the hall Redd joined in with a loud "Amen."

That's when the radio call came in to the reserve deputy. The news was relayed. The body of Viktor Karshenko had been found. Pastor Bob fell momentarily silent.

"Holy shit," he finally muttered, stumbling to his feet.

"Christ on a crutch," moaned the defrocked Reverend Redd Benson.

Word came the authorities were flying Karshenko's body, now referred to officially as "the remains," down from the mountain and hoped to have it at the county morgue within an hour. It was now dark, and the transfer had been difficult and dangerous; but the search team felt that they could not leave him up there through another night. The rest of the search party had gone up farther and had radioed the recovery team that they were camping for the night. The recovery team had been left behind and was working its way back down to the road. Viktor's body had been loaded onto the helicopter. It had lifted off and he was on his way back to civilization to whatever extent that would matter to him anymore.

"We're fucked," stated Redd. Pastor Bob nodded, his face gone slack at the thought of what this would mean to the conference and its future. And, worst of all, to his own future. All thought of holiness had been stripped away with the news. They could see the conferees now leaving in droves and, worse yet, asking for refunds of tuition and room and board money. Money that had already been spent, or was earmarked to pay the salaries for the Director and the Chaplain, among others. And then there was next year. How do you advertise and promote a conference when something like this could happen? It was hard enough as it was.

Pastor Bob wandered off to the kitchen to assuage his worry. Some left-over pasta from lunch would hit the spot. He had to keep his strength up. The kitchen help was cleaning up as he reheated the cold linguine and sat down to eat it. There wasn't a smile in the place. Some of the conferees were drinking stale, black coffee from a tall urn in the corner and whispering among themselves, glancing over at Pastor Bob from time to time.

Redd Benson was also contemplating his future. He thought he had hit bottom when he hired on here but clearly that was not the case. At least here he had been working and rehabilitating his resume. This was not going to help that effort at all. And then there was also the possibility now of an audit, especially if there were any questions about the finances and if people were demanding refunds. He had borrowed a small amount of cash a few weeks ago from the till, and had not yet had a chance to replace it and now, perhaps, no means to replace it. A mere thousand dollars, but still, it could get nasty. He had already had his day in court with the IRS and those bastards down in Texas. And worse yet, the CBS network crowd with their insatiable need for intrigue and scandal. He could just see the image of his face all across the TV screens of America again as they replayed those pedophile tapes over and over. The world was suddenly turning to shit. Again. He groaned audibly.

Meanwhile, back in the Eagle Cap wilderness, Russell was now wandering aimlessly. It was getting dark and he had no idea where he was or where he should be going. The path had divided and he just hoped he had taken the right one. Both of them seemed to be going up and that was all he knew to do: keep going up. The elevation gain was becoming steeper and steeper, but he pressed on. Night was falling quickly. For a brief moment he thought of Lucy and wondered how the old folks were doing. "Well, who gives a crap," he finally said out loud to no one in particular. And, indeed, there was no one in particular to hear him.

CHAPTER 49

JESSE AND BIG CAL, WITH CANDI NOW IN TOW, HAD FINALLY ARRIVED AT one of the small upper wilderness mountain lakes, nestled back in the trees. The landscape had flattened into an alpine meadow and the elevation remained fairly constant. It was dark when they arrived, but there was a full moon and the little lake lay quiet and serene. They set up the tent under some trees and Jesse built a small fire. There was a circle of charred rocks that previous campers had used and soon he had a blaze going. Jesse was surprised that he could get it going so easily. If it hadn't been so God-damned cold, the fire might have been nice. There were still patches of snow here and there, where even the mid-day sun couldn't reach, despite the fact that it was the middle of the summer. But Jesse was not thinking so much about his Nez Perce heritage anymore. His white man genes seemed to have kicked back in, somewhere back down the trail. It happened after he tripped and stumbled over a tree root, falling on his face into the brush and a bunch of nettles. Jesse was beginning to doubt his family history. He was still picking barbed stickers out of his cheeks, forehead and hands.

Candi was sullen and not willing to speak to either Cal or Jesse. She huddled in the back of the tent and refused to eat or talk. She did drink a swig of water. She glowered at them and finally had to speak her mind. "You shitheads have no idea what the hell you're doin'," she would snarl from time to time. She was in a real fix. She could try to take off, but where would she go? She had no idea where they were. It was cold. She had nothing to protect herself from the elements. When they had taken her she was just dressed for the conference, and not prepared to survive in the rugged wilderness. She could not imagine she could make it back to civilization under the circumstances. She would have to rely them and bide her time. Maybe she would be rescued somehow. She had seen a helicopter cruising over the mountain from time to time during the climb up. It had never come close, however, and Jesse had always forced her and Cal under a canopy of the trees until it had passed over.

Cal crawled into the tent and looked at her. She could see that he was uncomfortable with the situation. He always looked away whenever she looked directly at him.

"Cal," she said, "What the hell are you doin' getting mixed up in this? Remember our times at the club? You and me? We were always better than what went on there." She paused and bit her lip. "He's going to hurt me, Cal. You know that. Do you want that?" Cal said nothing and turned away, getting something out of his backpack. He didn't respond, but backed out of the tent.

That night, with the sky full of stars and the forest speaking to them in quiet, night noises, Candi tried to sleep. Despite her exhaustion, she was unable to do so. She just lay there on the hard, cold, lumpy ground, trying to figure out a plan that would save her from this situation. Jesse had rolled up in his mummy bag and was snoring away as if nothing was out of the ordinary. Maybe he really is a Nez Perce, thought Candi. She knew he was sleeping on his pistol. Any effort to take it from him would likely be futile.

Cal, too, was snoring like a chainsaw going through hard wood. His giant body was moving up and down, up and down. How could they sleep like this? Candi wondered. She thought she had heard a noise just outside the tent. She thought of bears. Or mountain lions. She knew she was stuck where she was. Jesse and Cal were both her captors and her protectors at the same time. What a shitty deal that is, she told herself. She thought of what had been her life and her hopes. She thought of her family and the fact that she might never see them again. For a long time she lay on her back staring up at the slanted ceiling of the small tent. Lying next to Cal, she could hear him groan and release a long, melancholy rumble of gas from time to time. It seemed an oddly apt commentary on her situation.

CHAPTER 50

THE NEXT MORNING SHERIFF WAIN WAS THE FIRST ONE UP. HE rousted the others.

"Time to hit the trail," he called to those still sleeping off the fatigue and aches of the previous day's trek. The men stirred and one by one they rose to meet the day and its challenges. They prepared a simple breakfast, packed their gear and resumed their ascent up the mountain trail. Already a helicopter was making passes back and forth. Radioed reports from the pilot and also from the search headquarters back at the conference site had revealed no new information. No one had yet been spotted.

They did receive a report by radio from the medical examiner's office that the autopsy of Viktor's body had not revealed any violent cause of death. It appeared he had had a massive heart attack. He had been, according to the pathologist, a heart attack waiting to happen.

Slowly the search party worked its way on up the trail. Little by little the cover of trees was thinning. From time to time they saw signs that someone had been there before them. There appeared to be fresh boot tracks in the dirt. Wain had seen a small lake on the map about another ten miles up. He hoped they could make it that far today. He had also noted that Russell Kees was no longer with them. Frankly, he was relieved that Kees was gone. Wain assumed that the professor had tired of the trek and turned back, realizing the hike was just too demanding. He's probably back at the Wallowa Lake Lodge eating a hearty breakfast and drinking Bloody

Marys, Wain thought. He could use a Bloody Mary himself about now. Little would he have guessed what Russell was actually doing at that moment.

Russell had actually left the search team's campsite and gone deeper into the dense underbrush of the forest. He was inept, to say the least. He had no pack, no gear, no food. He had spent the night huddled under a covering he had made of brush and fir boughs. He was rather proud of himself for having been able to do so. Oddly enough, he actually had gotten some sleep. Now it was morning. He listened intently for any sounds of either the searchers or Jesse and Cal. He heard nothing but the sounds of the forest speaking back to him. He was hungry and noticed berries on a bush. He began gathering them. They looked like huckleberries, he decided. They were tart but were enough to satisfy his immediate hunger. He had no water, however, and began looking for a stream of some sort. He could hear the soothing sound of water coursing over rocks and soon came upon a narrow stream. He lay down and drank. It was ice cold and delicious.

The sun was climbing in the sky and Russell could see the helicopter flying back and forth. He wondered about Candi. He wondered whether she was still even alive. He felt perhaps if he could locate Jesse and Cal himself, he could figure out a way to rescue her. The search party was just too slow and cumbersome. By the time they got up to the top, Candi could easily be dead - like Viktor. Time was of the essence. He had not thought of poor Lucy for several days now. She was on her own. As was he. In his own now somewhat mad, professorial way, he pressed on. He began to feel an invigoration he had never experienced before. He was one with nature. He felt truly alive. He felt like Rheinhold Zuber was speaking just to him.

Meanwhile Candi was getting increasingly agitated. Jesse was starting to come unglued as his effort to extort money out of Viktor and now their flight to avoid detection and arrest was all unraveling. Big Cal was also finally getting it through his thick head that the shit was hitting the fan, big time.

"What we doin' up here?" he asked Jesse, as they sat by the shore of the lake. "We got nothin' goin' for us here." He was picking at his teeth with a splinter of a stick he had picked up.

"Oh, shut the fuck up," groused Jesse. "If you can't help, at least keep your big fuckin' yap shut." He was smoking the last of his cigarettes. The pot had been comsumed long ago. What a lousy way to have to quit smoking, he thought. Cal had already smoked the last of his.

"What're we doin' up here?" Cal asked again. "We're goin' to get caught, for sure. I don't want to go to jail." He paused and looked over at Candi who was sitting in front of the tent and glaring at them. "And what about her?" He pointed to Candi. "What're we going to do about her? I don't want to see her hurt."

"Well, what can they do to us?" answered Jesse. "We didn't kill the old Russian. He just God-damned died on us. Maybe it was just his time." He paused to watch a fish leap up out from the calm surface of the lake, and make a splash as it reentered the water. "And Candi, hell, she won't rat on us. We didn't kidnap her."

"The hell you didn't," Candi yelled from her place in front of the tent. She came roaring down to where they were seated. "I'm going to hang your balls from the Empire State Building when this is all over."

Jesse stood and faced her. Just who the hell does she think she is? he thought, as she charged him, her face red with anger, her fists clenched, her arms waving wildly. Doesn't she know I'm Nez Perce? And she's nothin' but a God-damned farm girl! He was once again Jesse Red Hawk, Nez Perce. He ducked as she took a swing at him. He grabbed her arm as it whistled past his head and then jerked her around, pushing her arm up her back. She screamed with the pain of it.

"You'll keep your fuckin' mouth shut, or you'll be dead," Jesse growled. "Just like the old Russian."

Candi was sobbing, groans coming from deep inside, as she tried to escape from Jesse's grip. But she was not strong enough and the pain was too great. She was certain he was going to break her arm. Jesse took out his gun and pushed the barrel into her neck. "I could waste you right here, if I wanted to. You're no use to me now."

He almost grinned as he said it. He then let go of her arm and grabbed her long hair and yanked it back, hard. She screamed again. Then he jerked her down onto her knees into the loose gravel of the lakeshore and dug his knee into her back, her face ground into the stones and muck. He held the gun to the back of her head. "Fuck with me and you'll be dead," he hissed in her ear. His facial tic was working overtime.

It was the last thing Jesse would ever say or do. A huge shadow suddenly fell across him, like the sun being blotted out. A massive arm reached around his neck and snatched him up, off his feet, and away from Candi. Free, she fell to the ground. It was Big Cal. He had Jesse in a grip from which, despite his Nez Perce history, he could not and would not escape. Cal roared his anger at Jesse and tightened his hold. Jesse's face was turning from a deep red to an even deeper bluish purple as he gurgled and struggled to breathe, his arms flailing. Then Cal lifted him bodily off his feet and he held him clenched in his powerful arms, Jesse's feet dangling. The gun fell from his hand. Seconds later he suddenly went limp. Cal locked him in his iron grip for a minute longer, and then dropped him to the ground. Jesse lay there, motionless. Cal leaned over and picked up the pistol Jesse had dropped and stuck it in his belt.

Candi watched the scene with horror. Big Cal said nothing. He just looked down at Jesse, his face drained of emotion. Then he turned to Candi.

"You okay?"

She nodded and pointed at Jesse's body there on the ground. "You've killed him." She bent down and put a finger to his throat trying to find a pulse. There was none. She looked back up at Cal.

Big Cal nodded back. "Yeah," he said. "He was hurtin' you and maybe was goin' to kill you." He sucked a deep breath into his wide chest. He'd never actually killed another person before. "I couldn't let that happen." He paused. "I'm here to protect you. No matter what."

"Thank you, Cal." Candi sat down on a large rock and looked at him, surveyed the scene, stared down at Jesse. She knew he was right. Eventually Jesse would have had to do something about her. She was the one who could send him to prison for the rest of his life. She was the one who could rat him out. He had been increasingly erratic as he felt the law closing in on them. The helicopter had been passing overhead throughout the day. He had known the police were coming for them. It had been just a matter of time. And not much more of that. His dreams had turned to shit in his hands. If not at that particular moment, Candi knew, he would have had to kill her eventually. Or abandoned her to the wilderness where she surely would have died. Cal had saved her life. For all his stupidity and his bumbling ways, killer or not, he had saved her.

CHAPTER 52

THE SEARCHERS CONTINUED THEIR SLOW TREK UP THE MOUNTAINSIDE. The elevation gain was leveling out. The landscape was gradually flattening and becoming alpine, and the trees changed from tall fir to more slender lodgepole pine and were spaced farther apart. The vegetation was more stunted. Sheriff Wain was leading the way. They would stop from time to time to rest and take a swig of water from canteens that were now almost empty. And then they would move on. With the Russian dead - for whatever reason - they knew Jesse and Cal would be becoming more and more desperate. That could mean only one thing: Candi Summers was increasingly in danger. And they had to be very careful about how they approached the kidnappers when they did come upon them. Candi was, essentially, a hostage now. They would very likely try to use her to shield themselves.

Wain raised his hand to stop the line of searchers. He laid out his map on the ground and knelt down to check out their current location. He had been in contact with base and had been informed that no more phone calls had been received. Either they were now out of cell range, their battery had gone dead, or they simply had nothing more to say to them. Now that the Russian was dead, they were fugitives and on the run. Sheriff Wain had radioed the helicopter that they were to take no independent action if they spotted them but were simply to report their whereabouts.

"It looks like there is a small lake about a mile more up the trail," Wain announced. They gathered around him, looking down at the map. "I wouldn't be surprised if they are camped somewhere in that vicinity." He pointed to a small body of water on the map. "They need water, just as we do, and that would make an ideal site for them. From there they would have no choice but to climb farther up toward the alpine areas and they would be out in the open and easily spotted by the helicopter. Soon they will, in effect, have no place to run." He also pointed out where the Mt. Howard ski area was on the map and where the terminal for the tram was. "It is possible they might try to make it over there and escape back down to the highway. It would be a difficult and treacherous hike to get there." Wain grinned. "But like Ali once said, you can run, but you can't hide."

CHAPTER 53

I T WAS A SHORT TIME LATER THAT THE HELICOPTER PILOT FINALLY SPOTTED Big Cal and Candi, standing by the lake waving and waving. There was a clearing not far away and, after radioing the news and location to Sheriff Wain and getting his permission to land, they gently set the copter down. Wain advised them that the search team was not more than a mile away and was slowly but surely working its way toward the site.

A short time later Wain and the search team arrived at the lake. They found the helicopter with its rotors still turning and the pilot and crew standing with Big Cal and Candi. Immediately one of the searchers, a medical doctor from Enterprise, took Candi into the tent and gave her a quick physical exam to make sure she was all right. Then Wain went into the tent too and questioned her at length as to what had happened there. Jesse's body was still lying by the lake where Cal had dropped him, his face in death now mottled and gray. There was no longer any twitch. Photographs were taken of the crime scene and Wain and his investigators from the state police combed the area for any further clues or insight into what had happened there. Then they loaded Jesse's body onto the chopper to be transported eventually to Enterprise and the office of the medical examiner.

Two state police officers read Big Cal his Miranda rights and took him into custody. He did not resist. They handcuffed him and put him in the helicopter too. Candi climbed in after him. Up and away they went, over the treetops, cruising down toward the conference grounds far below. Candi could see that the search team now had turned around and was heading back toward the trailhead. She was grateful to be alive. Jesse had gone completely nuts. She was certain he would have killed her. Big Cal had saved her life. She looked over at him, silent, his massive body leaning against the far side of the cabin, his huge arms behind his back, his wrists bound together by the handcuffs. He was looking down, and out the window. His face was stoic and unreadable. What would be his future now? Candi wondered. He could very likely be going to prison for a long time. But he had saved her life. There had to be some reward for that.

The helicopter set down in a clearing near the parking lot of the tram. Police and some of the conference participants rushed forward to help. Sgt. Harvey got Cal out of the copter and put him into the back seat of a police cruiser. It was decided Candi should go to the emergency room at the hospital in Enterprise for a more thorough check up just to make sure she was okay, despite her assertions to the contrary. So she was taken away by a medic from the local fire department.

Viktor's body had been taken to the medical examiner's office and the autopsy had been done. As had been reported, it was determined that he had suffered a massive cardiac arrest. Clearly the exertion from the hike and the cold and dampness of the night in the wilderness had been too much for him. Redd Benson would have to locate the next of kin, if there were any, as well as notify the administration of Robarts College of the Ozarks to make arrangements for transfer of his remains. They would hold a memorial service at the Great Hall that evening. Pastor Bob was even now preparing his eulogy.

Sheriff Wain and the members of the search team who had been on the mountain finally returned to the conference center too. It was late in the day and supper was being prepared by the kitchen staff. The search team members were thanked for their efforts and disbanded. A number of them headed to the Round 'em Up to hash over the day's exciting events and unwind.

Dinner in the dining hall was subdued. The death of Viktor had been a severe blow to the congeniality of the group. No one had known him well, but everyone had been touched by him in some way, and stories were circulating among the diners of how he had affected their lives, even in that short time, whether true or not.

Candi was checked out at the ER and released as the emergency room doctors were unable to find any significant injuries. Bruises and scrapes were the only signs of her ordeal. She was given some sleeping pills to help her rest, and some pain medications for the aches and pains she still had from Jesse's assault and the strenuous trek into the wild.

No one as yet had missed Russell. No one realized he was, perhaps, still out there somewhere there somewhere off in the wilderness and that he had not returned with the other searchers.

That evening during the memorial service for Viktor, Candi looked around for him and he was nowhere to be found. Where could Russell be," she wondered? Perhaps he had returned home to Oregon City. Perhaps he had already left and gone back to the grim-faced woman whose photo sat on his desk.

CHAPTER 54

RUSSELL WAS ACTUALLY TRYING HIS BEST TO SLEEP UNDER A TREE. HE had eaten some more berries and drunk some more water from the stream nearby. He had again made a bed of fir boughs, and they were not too uncomfortable. Their sweet odor was actually quite nice. He had tried to strike out on his own in search of Candi, in the vain and improbable hope of rescuing her from Jesse and Cal. In doing so he had simply become lost. Ill equipped as he was for the great outdoors, he was now beginning to feel a sense of panic. The helicopters had stopped passing over. He had hoped to attract the attention of one of the pilots, but now it appeared this wasn't going to happen. There was only silence all around him. The forest seemed to be closing in on him.

The next morning Russell gathered some more berries and slurped down some more water from the stream. To his surprise, he found himself slowly beginning to actually enjoy himself. He had never really been much of an outdoorsman. He hadn't belonged to the Boy Scouts. He had never been in the military. He had never been a hunter or a camper and he knew little about wilderness survival. He had grown up in an urban setting and his parents never took him out into the world of nature, other than city parks. But he had to acknowledge that the solitude was somewhat pleasant. Little by little, he felt the stress of modern life leaving his body. No more East Hills Liberty College, with its boring students, except, for Candi - and his even more boring colleagues. And even no more Lucy. He hadn't quite realized how dull and uninteresting their marriage had become. In fact, had always been. With no children to raise they had few interests in common anymore. They had grown apart. Of course there was still his writing, his poetry. But alone here in the great outdoors, with no one to impress he had to admit he really didn't think he was all that good at it and the world could probably get along quite nicely without his offerings. "*Ode to the Salvation of a Woodcock*" just might be his best and only lasting contribution to literature.

A certain sense of happiness, indeed, elation, was starting to manifest itself somewhere deep in his spirit. He felt a certain sense of liberation. Freedom now! Freedom now! The words of Martin Luther King, Jr. rang in his mind. He was free, free at last. He thought of the words of Zuber: the power of the moment. For perhaps the first time in his adult life, he felt truly free. No one knew where he was. And maybe, at this point, no one cared. Perhaps he could still find Candi, and maybe she would agree with him that life here in the wilderness was where they should be. Not confined to a life of norms and demands and impossible standards. They would start a new civilization free of the idiosyncrasies of the so-called modern world, with its wars, famine, ignorance and blight. They would be beholden to no one, the subjects of no one. He recalled a line from a poem by Tennyson: "My friends, 'tis not too late to seek a newer world." The thought was beginning to appeal to him more and more. Perhaps he could make a newer world. Right here in the Eagle Cap Wilderness. But first he needed to find Candi, the idealized Eve to his idealized Adam.

CHAPTER 55

THE NEXT MORNING RUSSELL STILL HAD NOT MADE AN APPEARANCE. No one had seen him since mid-day the day before when he had been on the mountainside as part of the search team. No one remembered whether or not he had returned with them. He simply wasn't anywhere to be found. The cabin where he and Viktor had been billeted still held all of his belongings. Nothing had been disturbed as far as anyone could tell. The authorities assumed that he must still be somewhere in the Eagle Cap Wilderness. So another search party was formed, this one much less enthusiastic than the previous day. Searching for a professor was not nearly as much fun - and potentially rewarding as searching for a foreign dignitary and a stripper. But off they went, back to the trailhead and on up the mountain, looking for poor Russell.

But Russell had decided he did not want to be found any longer. He had found his paradise, much to his surprise. By mid-day he heard the sounds of the search team tramping through the brush and trees. He heard them calling his name. But he did not respond. Instead, he moved deeper and deeper into the depths of the forest, not up into the alpine areas but down, and into the darkness of the thick undergrowth where he could not be seen.

The team searched for several more days without success. Russell was not to be found even with the aid of the helicopters flying back and forth. And so, after several days, the search was abandoned. Either Russell was no longer in the wilderness area or something had happened to him. Perhaps he had been attacked by wolves, a bear or a mountain lion. In any event, there was no trace of him. The rescue team disbanded and the men went back home and back to their daily lives.

In the meantime Jesse's body had been taken to the country morgue where an autopsy was performed. The coroner's report said he had died of a massive crushing of his chest and larynx. What could have done that, no one seemed to know. The coroner said it would have had to have been some creature of great strength. There were no other injuries to the body, so it was not thought to have been a wild animal. Sheriff Wain had interviewed both Candi and Cal, but neither of them could account for it.

Wain had his suspicions but he had no evidence as to what might have actually taken place. But Big Cal just grunted and Candi said she had been taken against her will and that she didn't care that he was dead. She said he had threatened her with a gun and that she was sure he would have killed her if any attempt had been made to rescue her. Big Cal had been taken into custody on suspicion of murder pending consideration by the Wallowa County Grand Jury. The local district attorney for Wallowa County took the matter to the grand jury but, following Candi's testimony, they refused to return an indictment against Cal. As a result no formal charges were ever brought and Cal was released. Candi had testified before the grand jury that Cal had also been coerced into participating in the scheme by Jesse and had not exercised free will. She further testified that if Cal hadn't protected her Jesse likely would have killed her. A short time later Big Cal was finally released from the Wallowa County jail and Candi met him driving his old Honda Civic. They had hopes of convincing Gordie Nockers to give Cal his old job back. Candi had not realized her dream of becoming a Christian romance writer and decided she would just resume dancing for the time being. Christian romance could come later.

Jesse' body was finally sent to a mortuary in Oregon City where his bereaved and befuddled parents arranged a good Catholic Mass of Requiem. They had never understood him and his need to be an Indian. Thus ended Jesse's chaotic Nez Perce adventure. His gravestone would read simply "Jesse Irving Zaferelli. R.I.P."

CHAPTER 56

REDD BENSON HAD FALLEN INTO A DEEP DEPRESSION. HIS DREAMS OF his personal redemption had been crushed. The entire conference had gone down the shithole, as far as he was concerned. His board of directors was raising hell with him, as if the debacle was all, somehow, his fault. How could he be responsible for the fact that a pair of nut cases had grabbed the old Russian, who was also a nut case - and carted him off into the wilderness to die? How could he have predicted that? Or that they would take one of the students with them? Hells, bells, he was not a psychic. He couldn't see into the future. Already the TV stations and some newspaper reporter from the La Grande Observer were hanging around, asking embarrassing questions. A station in Portland had even dug up the old footage of his troubles with CBS and the charges of his being a pedophile. His face was being rebroadcast all over the country. Redd could see he was not destined to be the director of God+Write much longer. He looked over at Pastor Bob, who was preparing his farewell sermon, a profound lesson on lechery and sodomy, two subjects close to his heart.

"What the fuck we goin' to do now?" Redd asked. He somehow hoped Pastor Bob had all the answers. "This shit trap is fallin' down around our ears."

"Your ears, I might say." Pastor Bob stared at him." We must try to remain calm and trust in the Lord," he added. "I'd suggest we pray on it, Brother Redd."

"Fuck you," muttered "Brother" Redd. "You pray on it if you want to." With that he got up and poured a cup of coffee from the pot that had been sitting there on the hot plate for at least an hour. He winced as he took a swig of the black tar.

"Whoee, this stuff tastes like diarrhea shit."

"Please, Redd, mind your language," answered Pastor Bob. "I am still a man of the cloth, after all. Show some respect." He paused. "And so were you." He smiled benevolently. "At one time."

Redd Benson gave him the finger and sat back down at his desk.

The students were leaving in droves. Two of the instructors had already left when their paychecks were rejected at the bank, another was dead and another had just disappeared, period. With old Viktor's busted heart also went any hopes for a nice, fat endowment. Who would have thought the old fart was ready to croak? Redd hadn't even had time to chat with him about maybe remembering them in his Will. And now his bucks would go to someone or somewhere else. Students were demanding their tuition money back. The instructors who were still there were now demanding payment in cash. Even the camp staff was getting restless and giving him stern looks whenever he went into the kitchen or the laundry room.

Pastor Bob leaned over and patted Redd on his knee. And then, quite unexpectedly, he left his hand on Redd's knee. Redd looked puzzled for a moment. He had never experienced such a show of affection or concern from Pastor Bob before. In fact, they hardly knew one another. Were it not for God+Write, they probably would never have crossed paths. He looked up. Pastor Bob had a most deified look on his round, sweating face. Redd, in his confusion, made no effort to remove Pastor Bob's blob of a hand. In fact, he found it rather comforting. He then hesitantly reciprocated and placed his own hand on top of Pastor Bob's. He needed all the reassurance he could get. Pastor Bob smiled his best Pastor Bob smile. Redd smiled back.

"I think it is all going to work out in the end," murmured Pastor Bob. "We must only trust in the one true God." He smiled again. "Shall we pray?"

197

CHAPTER 57

Candi had met Cal at the county jail just as he was being released. He had given her the keys to his old Honda, and she had driven over to Enterprise to get him. She felt the need to protect and take care of Cal now that he was her benefactor and had saved her life. She had always valued him at the club, whenever he took care of some pissant who was bothering her and not paying for the privilege. Back then she had seen him as just a big dumb friend, at best. But for a man so large, he could be very quick when the circumstances called for it. And he was loyal. She had always admired those qualities in him.

So now she had checked out of God + Write, along with many of the other students. It looked like the place was shutting down. The charter bus had been cancelled and everyone was on his or her own. Some of the participants were car-pooling with others to get back to the Portland area, or wherever it was they were heading. There was an air of confusion that was palpable about the place. For all the praying and singing of songs of praise, everything had all turned to shit. Pastor Bob and Redd Benson were nowhere to be found.

With Cal now at the wheel the creaking Honda chugged its way back toward Portland, the black clouds of smoke trailing out behind. They stopped in La Grande for a quick bite to eat at a fast food joint. Then they proceeded on, through Pendleton and west to the Columbia River, which they followed finally into the Portland area. Between the two of them they had less than fifty dollars to cover gas and any more meals they might need. For a vacation, this had turned into a pile of crap, thought Candi. But it had been an adventure, nonetheless. She had stared out of the window at the Grande Ronde River flowing past. Her return to the places of her youth had not been what she had expected. She wondered if Russell Kees had returned to the conference or if he had simply gone home too. Everywhere they had stopped in Wallowa County and Union County the happenings in the Eagle Cap Wilderness were on everyone's tongues. In the fast food place in La Grande one guy sitting next to them asked if they had heard the news. He said it had been reported that one guy might still up there on the mountain but the searchers had finally given up any hope of finding him alive. The man said he was a professor of some sort. A poet. He smirked when he said it.

That has to be Russell, thought Candi, munching on a french fry she had just dipped into a small cup of catup. What a shame. She took another bite of the french fry. He was such a nice guy, in his older guy sort of way, she thought. Even if she hadn't really understand a word of his poetry. But, she had to admit, he had been published. That had to count for something. But then she turned to Cal. She was seeing her hero in a new light. The big lug, she thought.

CHAPTER 58

SHERIFF JON WAIN SAT IN HIS POLICE CRUISER IN THE PARKING LOT OF Dinty's Burgers eating his dinner of a Doublepounder with cheese and bacon, two large orders of fries and a giant sized slurpy. He was alone, musing about the events of the past several days. His department had had more excitement in three days than he had experienced since being elected sheriff. He was disappointed that he could not nail Big Cal, and that Jesse had not lived to be prosecuted. The locals would have nailed his sorry ass to the nearest fence post, of which there were many. But Zaferelli had met his inevitable, but painful, end at the hands of Big Cal; of that much Wain was certain, even if he couldn't prove it. The case had been a crushing defeat for the justice system, one might say. He chuckled at his own joke as he wiped his chin to keep the special sauce from dripping down onto his tie. Technically he was off duty. But as sheriff, he knew he was never really off duty in fact. Such was the downside of being sheriff. But still, he could soon head for home, take off the uniform and perhaps wander over to the Round 'em Up for a few beers and a game of pool. Maybe even Gloria would be on duty. She just might want to come home with him once she closed up the place. She always said she liked the little guys. "Little man, big prick," she had once told him. "Just a law of nature. God's payback for being short."

The radio crackled static at him. Shit, he thought. I'm off duty. Still he responded. " Yeah? I'm headin' home."

It was Harvey.

"There's been a domestic beef over at the Larson place. Old man Larson was at it again. Beatin' up on the little woman. She finally got tired of it and just clubbed him with a big iron fry pan and he's now in bad shape at the E.R. Got a concussion, according to the doc. Lucky to still have his head. We took her into custody. We didn't want to but we had to. You know the law on that."

"I know," said Duke Wain.

"Thought you ought to know about it."

"Okay," he answered. "But I'm headin' home. File what you need to. I feel a hot shower comin' on. Don't bother me again unless it's murder or rape. I'm off to see Gloria at the Round 'em Up." He paused to let that last comment sink in. "If you get my drift." He smiled.

He could hear the chuckling on the other end. Grinning like a teenager in heat, he signed off, turned off his radio, finished off his fries, and took the final bite of the double burger with cheese and bacon. He got out of the police car and slowly walked over to the trash can, tossed his food wrappers into the bin, returned to the car, got in and started up the motor. It roared to life. Sucking in the last of his slurpy, he slowly pulled out of the parking lot into traffic, the events of the last few days already beginning to recede to the back of his mind. Thoughts of Gloria took their place. He smiled. She was one fine woman. Maybe she'd even be wearing her "rodeo" bra.

Little man, big prick! What's better than a man in uniform.

CHAPTER 59

THE FIRST LOVE WEDDING CATHEDRAL, IN LAS VEGAS, NEVADA WAS truly lovely. It was decorated like a miniature Graceland, complete with decorative guitars covering the walls and a constant sound track of Elvis himself singing all of his famous hits. The resident minister and owner, the Reverend Dr. Corbin L. Jones Jr., was always immaculately dressed in his best Elvis suit, the white polyester one with fake diamonds sewn in long rows on all the seams. His dyed black hair was long and swept back like the King's, greasy and thick; his sideburns almost came down to his chin line. He had long ago begun to wear an inexpensive hairpiece he got through the Dr. Leonard mail order catalog to cover the growing bald spot on the crown of his head. Truth be told, he looked more like Elvis looked when he was closing in on death than the younger Elvis whose sultry good looks had entranced an entire generation of women fans. Bloated and lumpy, he wore the suit like a sausage. It took both him and Mrs. Corbin L. Jones, Jr. a good deal of time each morning just to get him into it. And once it was on, it was on for the duration. He could still get the zipper down if he needed to relieve himself, but that was it. It took both of them to zip it back up without causing major damage to his privates.

Corbin and his wife had invested in The First Love Wedding Cathedral some ten years earlier, after Corbin's unfortunate venture with the used car lot in Needles, California. He had had to go into bankruptcy. He had been buying fleet cars from insurance salvage companies and rental car companies and spinning the odometers back a few thousand miles and selling them as pristine and low mileage. The state attorney general had finally shut him down and he declared bankruptcy soon after that. The "Cease and Desist" Order from the attorney general made it almost impossible for him to start another business in the great State of California.

So when the opportunity arose to turn an old '76 gas station into the wedding chapel, he took it. Corbin had always been handy with his hands, so it wasn't long before they were ready for business. And the business came rolling in. Drunks, lounge lizards of all sorts, ex-cons and meth addicts from all over the known world came in to get hitched. Corbin had obtained a ministerial license for twenty dollars from a mail-order seminary in Kansas he had found on-line, and he was set to go. The Elvis theme had been his wife's idea. She had always loved Elvis. That there were a dozen or more similar Elvis operations in the heart of Las Vegas did not deter her or Corbin. There was always room for one more Elvis.

And so it was that a young couple arrived at their door wanting the usual - a wedding, pronto. The young man was the size of a house. Broad and ugly as a Brahma bull, he appeared to be about as smart. The young woman was, surprisingly, quite pretty and said she had been a college student someplace in Oregon. Candice was her name. The brute of a man went by the name of Cal. They seemed an unlikely couple, but Corbin had seen worse. Much worse. And much stranger. He rememberd only last week the Sri Lankan snake charmer and his girl friend. They had insisted on having their pet boa constrictor serve as the best man. And, Corbin opined privately, that couple would probably be looking for a divorce lawyer before the week was up anyway. "What happens in Vegas, stays in Vegas." That's what everyone always said. So what did it matter? If folks had the marriage license and the money (no checks accepted), he had the ministerial license and needed the money and he was there to make the wedding happen. It was all perfectly legit. He felt he was doing God's work.

While Mrs. Corbin L. Jones, Jr. pumped away on the second-hand Hammond organ ("Love me Tender" as the prelude) and Big Cal waited expectantly at the altar with the Reverend Dr. Jones, Jr., Candice came tripping slowly down the aisle. She held a bouquet of dusty fake roses in her hands, courtesy of the wedding chapel. The chapel had also provided the now off-white full-length ill-fitting wedding gown. Within a matter of minutes the vows were exchanged, the newly weds kissed, and Big Cal slipped a genuine ring of almost real rolled gold onto the young lady's finger. He had purchased it the day before at a Rite-Aid drug store in the outskirts of Las Vegas. Mrs.Jones burst forth with a loud and raucous upbeat version of "You Ain't Nothin' But A Hounddog" and the deed was done. The happy couple paid their bill and fled in an aging Honda Civic that was soon lost from sight in the clouds of black smoke pouring from the back end.

Corbin and Mrs. Jones smiled after them like new parents watching their offspring leaving home for the first time. They took great satisfaction in bringing couples like this together in holy matrimony, even if only briefly. Truly another marriage made in heaven. But that was one ugly dude, thought the Reverend Dr. Corbin L. Jones, Jr. as they drove away. One really ugly dude.

The Reverend Dr. Jones, however, quickly pocketed the cash and headed over to the roulette tables at the mini-casino next door, adjacent to the 711 store. He was feeling lucky that day. Very lucky.

CHAPTER 60

NIGHT WAS FALLING AND THE FOREST WAS DEEPENING INTO SHADOW when Russell returned to the small stone hut that had now become his home. He had spread pine boughs on the dirt floor and had managed to build a fire in the fire pit, having discovered he could spark a flame and light dried pine needles from pieces of flint he had found scattered about the area. He had seen natives in far off places doing just that on National Geographic shows on TV. From the stream he had actually caught a fish. To be sure, it was small and there wasn't much meat on it, but there was some. He had skewered it with a stick and held it over the flames. And it had tasted marvelous. The very best fish he had ever eaten. Together with the berries he had gathered from nearby bushes, and cold, cold delicious water from the stream, it had been a wonderful meal. Perhaps the best meal he had had in years.

Russell felt like a king here in the wild, dependant for the first time in his entire life only on himself for survival. He felt an inner strength he had never known before. He felt freedom. He found himself reveling in the power of the moment. He thought back on his having read sections of old Reinhold Zuber's, *The Power of the Moment*. According to the blurbs on the cover, he recalled that Zuber had made a fortune with the book. At one time Russell would have sneered at such a notion as the power of the moment, although he would certainly envied Zuber's monetary success with the book. But Zuber had been right. Russell had never experienced such ecstasy. He lay back and looked up at the starry night, visible through the opening in the hut wall that served as a window. Those stars were up there only for him, he thought. That full moon, with illuminated clouds drifting casually across its face, was there only for him. He was the only human being left on the face of the earth.

There had been no more helicopters passing overhead now for several days. Russell assumed they were no longer looking for him. He was certain that he could hike out whether and whenever he wished but for now he was beginning to realize this might just be the life he had always wanted. An early retirement, in a sense. He turned that thought slowly over and over in his mind as he nibbled away, getting the last shred of meat off of a small fish bone. He then casually picked his teeth with the bone, content and sated. Somewhere in the distance wolves were howling. It didn't bother him in the least. The old Russell would have been terrified. But not the new Russell. The new Russell felt the strength of all native history in his blood. He was finally living the life he was intended to live. There would be no more East Hills Liberty College. Or any college, for that matter. No more dull existence with Lucy, each day a repeat of the last, uninteresting and totally predictable. No, he would not miss his students either, except, perhaps for Candi. Nor would he miss any of his colleagues. Or those assholes in the administration office, always sending out inane memos insisting that he attend their pray services or committee meetings. Yes, he thought, if Candi were only here everything would be truly perfect. They could restart the world together. They would be the new Adam and Eve. In a new Garden of Eden. However now it seemed that was not to be. But perhaps she was out there still, looking for him too. Now at peace, he wrapped himself in the softness of pine boughs and lay down by the dying fire. Soon, he thought, he would be deep in sleep, dreaming of his new life. He would grow his hair long and live as God had truly intended. Then, with a sudden, overwhelming sense of his new freedom, he leapt to his feet and tore the ridiculous hairpiece from the crown of his head, stepped out of the hut and threw it as far as he could, out into the darkness of the forest night, never to be seen again. Yes, this was truly the power of the moment.

CHAPTER 61

THE HONEYMOON WAS TRULY IDYLLIC. THE DRIVE FROM NEVADA AND across southern California, through Bakersfield and now finally down into Los Angeles was wonderful. It was everything they could have hoped for. Neither Big Cal nor Candi had ever been out of Oregon before. So this was the trip of a lifetime for both of them. First had come the long drive down to Las Vegas and now they were about to enter Los Angeles. La La land, some folks called it. It was the world of celebrities that they had both heard so much about. It couldn't get any better than this. They had even spent their first night as a married couple in a Motel Six in Barstow. It had been truly heavenly.

And now Los Angeles lay before them like the smog-ridden metropolis it is. A dirty, yellowish layer of gunk lay over the city like a long, disgusting blanket. Soon they were submerged in it, coughing like natives. But their thoughts were only of Hollywood and all the movie and television stars they would soon see roaming the streets. Wilshire Boulevard. Beverly Hills, Rodeo Drive. The site of these fabled places was all too much. They found a modest motel in Santa Monica, an Econo-Lodge, and quickly settled in. The motel even provided a continental breakfast, free of charge with the price of the room. And it had a swimming pool. With a coupon they found in a roadside brochure, the room cost only sixty-nine dollars a night, plus tax. They had both gotten advances reluctantly from Gordie Nockers, so the room was worth every penny. It was even better, thought Cal, than that motel in Joseph; and that one had been pretty damned good.

And then Cal produced the big surprise he had been promising Candi ever since they left Las Vegas. Proudly, and for Cal, with great ceremony, he presented an envelope to her. It was one he had taken from the motel room desk in Barstow. She opened it hesitantly, somewhat bewildered. To her surprise, inside were two tickets to attend the next day's taping of the Larry Singer Show. The real, honest to God, actual, real, Larry Singer Show. Right there in good old Los Angeles, California. The center of the known universe. Cal had been busting his buttons in an effort to keep it a secret.

While she had to admit to herself that her excitement over the tickets was nowhere near the excitement displayed by Big Cal, who, despite his bulk, was literally dancing about the room, she felt like she was now truly part of the celebrity crowd and as though she would soon be rubbing shoulders with the likes of Joan Rivers and Erik Estrada. It was all so overwhelming. And Cal had been so sweet. She had never imagined that beneath that big, dumb-looking outer bulk of a man was this sweet-hearted little boy. He was truly the man of her dreams. And he had been right there in front of her all this time. He had been watching over her at the club protecting her from Jesse on the mountain, willing to kill for her if necessary. If he wanted to see the Larry Singer Show, so did she.

CHAPTER 62

THE NEXT MORNING THEY GOT TO THE TELEVISION STUDIO EARLY. THEY wanted the best seats they could get. Already, however, there was a lineup at the door. It stretched all the way around the corner of the building. It was an odd looking group of people, even to Cal. Apparently the theme of the day was one-legged female Episcopal priests who had married and been unfaithful to one armed Eastern European men, with a few dysfunctional ex-con couples displaying their prison tattoos mixed in to liven up the proceedings for the redneck audience. Cal was in seventh heaven. He watched with wonder as the prospective guests and their entourages arrived in stretch limos, stumbling and hobbling past, some hanging onto walkers, some leaning on canes or crutches, into the studio, and off into the inner recesses of the green rooms. It was going to be one hell of a bang-up show. Cal was certain of that. His dreams were about to be realized. He hoped to get Larry's autograph, right there in person. Not just some automated signature like the one he had on the wall of his trailer at home. To meet Larry Singer face to face would be too much.

At 9 a.m. sharp the doors opened and the spectators, pushing and shoving, were ushered briskly into the studio. They sat for a brief while just watching the show being set up for the shoot. A man wearing a headset and holding a mike came out on stage to warm up the crowd. No one paid much attention to him, however. He wasn't Larry Singer, after all. Soon he was replaced by the well-built men in black pants and T-shirts who maintained control of the participants and the spectators whenever they got out of line. Cal thought how he'd love to have that job. To hell with Nockers' Up-Town Bar and Grille. The fun was about to begin. The lights began to dim. The stage floodlights came on.

Somewhere off stage an announcer's voice blared out an introduction, and then, suddenly, there he was. LARRY SINGER himself. Larry Singer in the flesh, mike in hand, tousled brownish blonde hair falling down gently across his forehead in an almost boyish way. Although he looked a bit older then he did on television, it was the real Larry Singer. Big Cal thought he was going to faint. After a short recap about the show's topic, it was time to bring out the first guest of the day and to hear her tale of woe. A tall, skinny, gothic looking woman in black wearing a clerical collar came through the curtain and stumbled her way onto the stage, her one leg and a crutch holding her up. She was, perhaps, fifty years old, had long, black, slicked hair, and blackened makeup. She said her name was Reverend Thelma. She said that she had lost her right leg at the hip years ago when she was just a kid, in a threshing machine accident on the family farm in Wyoming. She took her time and tearfully related the sordid details of the bloody accident to the delight of the audience that hooted and hollared its disdain. She told how, at the scene of the accident, her severed leg had suddenly been snatched by an overzealous German shepherd that lived on a neighboring farm and how the dog had run away with it and how the dog and her leg were never seen again. And then she launched into her tale of a misbegotten romance with a one-armed merchant seaman from Bellerus named Anton, and described how he had used and abused her. They had met at a Buddhist retreat on the Aguas Caliente Indian Reservation outside of Palm Springs a couple of years before she had turned to the Episcopalian faith. The final blow to their relationship came when he left her for an obese quadriplegic woman from Thailand, just before Reverend Thelma was to give birth to their only child, Roger. At that point the crowd had been whipped into an absolute frenzy and Larry then, with a dramatic wave of his hand, the lock of his hair flopping up and down on his forehead, introduced Anton, who came rushing out of the green room waving his one arm to the hissing and further vilification of the audience. Anton immediately yelled curses at Reverend Thelma in his thick Eastern European accent and she came back at him. "Bastard." "Fuck Up!" she yelled, to the delight of all. That'll all get bleeped out, thought Cal, as they faced off at each other. Suddenly Anton screamed "Bitch" and "Whore" at Reverend Thelma

Then Reverend Thelma ran at him and almost took a flier off the stage, however, when her crutch got caught in the hem of her long dress. Anton charged her and the men in black had to rush in and separate the two of them and hold them at bay. The crowd was coming unglued. In the process of restraining Reverend Thelma, the front of her dress fell open and her scrawny breasts flopped out, much to the pleasure of everyone. That'll be blurred out, thought Cal, as he clapped and clapped, chanting loudly with the crowd, knowing he had finally seen for himself what all the others at home watching on their TV sets would never get to see, but always wanted to see - bare tits. That he had seen bare tits every night of the week at Nockers' Up-Town Bar and Grille, and Candi's in particular, didn't seem to register with him.

When the two had finally been separated the obese quadripeligic "other woman," the lady from Thailand was wheeled out onto the stage and the hooting started all over again. She lay in her chair staring at the ceiling lights and saying nothing much of anything. Larry asked her questions and tried his best to extract some sleazy information from her, but she was unresponsive. Clearly he was annoyed. What the hell was she doing here? he must have been thinking. He'd have to have a talk to the staff about this one. Apparently her knowledge of English was nonexistent and she was deaf to boot.

All in all, however, for Cal it was a glorious morning. It was the best day of his life, for sure. Even better than the wedding or their first night together in the motel in Barstow. Here he was in the heart of good old Hollywood, California at the Larry Singer Show with Candi at his side, and now his wife. Finally, as the show was drawing to its inevitable and disruptive climax, Cal leaned over to Candi, and smiled his Big Cal, stupid smile. Then he whispered in her ear.

"I didn't tell you this before, honeybuns, because I wanted it to be another big surprise for you." He then grinned mischievously, a truly happy man. He reached deep into the inside pocket of his new red checked blazer, bought just for the occasion, and presented Candi with yet another envelope. "I also got us tickets for tomorrow's taping of the season finale of "The Biggest Loser.""

THE END

RONALD TALNEY

R ONALD TALNEY WAS BORN in British Columbia but has lived in Oregon most of his life. He is an attorney retired from a private, non-profit legal aid program. In addition to a juvenile mystery novel, *The Ghost of Deadman's Hollow,* he is the author of five books of poems, most recently, *A Secret Weeping of Stones, New and Selected Poems,* from Plain View Press (2010) as well as numerous articles, personal essays, and individual poems in a variety of journals, literary magazines, newspapers and quarterlies. He lives in Lake Oswego, Oregon with his wife, Linnette.

Photo by Linnette Talney

CPSIA information can be obtained at www.ICGtesting.com
Printed in the USA
244992LV00005B/1/P

9 781592 996520